BLACK BOY WHITE SCHOOL

BRIAN F. WALKER

HARPER TEEN

An Imprint of HarperCollinsPublishers

HarperTeen is an imprint of HarperCollins Publishers.

Black Boy / White School
Copyright © 2012 by Brian F. Walker

Library of Congress Cataloging-in-Publication Data
Walker, Brian F.
  Black boy/white school / Brian F. Walker. — 1st ed.
    p. cm.
  ISBN 978-0-06-191483-6
  [1. Identity—Fiction. 2. African Americans—Fiction. 3. Race relations—
Fiction. 4. Preparatory schools—Fiction. 5. High schools—Fiction.
6. Schools—Fiction. 7. Maine—Fiction.] I. Title.
PZ7.W15216Bl 2012   2011016608
[Fic]—dc23   CIP
                                                                               AC

Typography by Erin Fitzsimmons
11 12 13 14 15   LP/RRDH   10 9 8 7 6 5 4 3 2 1
❖
First Edition

For Ava and Olivia

ONE

ANTHONY JONES, AN INKY-BLACK KNOT OF A fourteen-year-old, stomped down the elevated railroad tracks, hammering his thigh with a clenched fist. Inside his hand was crammed the hastily written note he had scribbled while his mother dictated. He'd been back at home only minutes before, splayed on the couch with one eye on the clock and the other on the TV, waiting for her key to stab the lock. She'd blown in and up the stairs, then slid out of her overcoat and barked the familiar orders: "Get up. I need you to go to the store."

Of course she did. And of course he went, just like the day before and the day before that. He wouldn't mind so much if she spread it around a little, maybe made his brothers go every now and then. But that would never happen. Andre and Darnell were too old to be bossed around and too big to hit.

"Maxi pads," he spat at the wooden ties in front of him. "What I look like, buyin' somebody's maxi pads?" He uncurled his fingers and reread the list, each printed item giving the paper weight. Two bags of shit, maybe three. How was he supposed to lug all of that by himself? "Whatever I cain't carry I'm just gon' leave," he said, and then checked over his shoulder. His mother had a way of showing up in unexpected places.

He scooped a handful of rocks and stomped on, looking for something or someone to hit. Some people called him a troublemaker, but he saw himself as more of an adventurer. The noise and the rush, the fear of getting caught, bitten, or beaten made him tease dogs and test total strangers, break bottles wherever he found them, and dash into the path of moving traffic.

"Maxi pads." The words made him uncomfortable, especially the first one. He tried to clear his head by firing a rock at a pole. It struck the wood with a *thok* and ricocheted into dead bushes. "She make me go to that school, she gon' have to get her own damn Kotex, anyway."

He checked behind him again and walked on, looking down at the houses and busy streets below. It was warm, more than sixty-five degrees in early March, and it looked like everybody in East Cleveland had found a reason to be outside. Dudes in T-shirts and baggy jeans slopped soap on Oldsmobiles and Mustangs, while packs of teenage girls walked by slowly, hoping for a chance to ignore them. Shorties on BMX bikes jumped curbs and toiled across the clumpy little lawns, flinging mud into the air behind them and drawing brown scars on the pavement. And packs of grim boys weighed down some of the street corners, flagging cars and leaning into the windows.

At a bridge he came down and crossed the street, pushed through the electric door at Judd's Supermarket, and found an empty cart. As he maneuvered the cart through the cramped and pitted aisles, Anthony wondered what it would take to get his mother to forget about Belton Academy. He wasn't going. They hadn't even given him an answer yet, and even if he did get in, he still wasn't going. Tuition was steep and his family was always broke.

That didn't stop his mother, though. All she could do was talk about it; tell her friends that her baby boy was going off to some "school for smart people" up in Maine. To hear her tell it, that dude from Belton came down to East Cleveland specifically looking for him. Never mind that he was a regular in detention. Never mind that he only once made the honor roll. And never mind that he didn't play organized sports, didn't belong to any clubs, and only occasionally finished his homework. He'd filled out the application, so now he was special.

And now he couldn't listen to music or talk on the phone without her jumping all over him about what they listened to up in Maine, or how they talked up in Maine, or how he better not go up to Maine and start acting ghetto. Maine. Anthony's mother didn't even know where it was until he'd shown it to her on a map, but that still didn't stop her from acting like she was born there.

His cart loaded, Anthony coasted to a stop in line, rested his elbows on the handle, and stared at the lanky security guard in front. Kids in the neighborhood called him Barney, even though that probably wasn't his real name. And every time he walked into the store, especially if he was with his best friends, Floyd and Mookie, Barney became their white shadow.

Anthony paid the cashier and accepted the change, dropped the money in his pocket, and lifted the bags. Walking out, he felt Barney's eyes on the back of his neck; felt like turning around and spitting.

Walking home, he came across a group of dope boys on the sidewalk. They were all wearing loosely laced Timberlands and blue hats or bandannas. One of them, chocolate brown with thin eyebrows and thick lips, smiled at him. "W'sup, Ant?" he said, and lightly punched the boy on the shoulder. "Yo' momma sent you to the store again, nigga? What you got in there?" He tried to look, but Anthony took a step back. Shane was cool but unpredictable.

Just then an old Ford rattled to a stop at the curb and a woman stuck her wild hair out the window. Shane stood tall and checked the block, then he pimp-limped over to the car. Seconds later, he was back at his spot on the corner, adding a crumpled bill to the knot of cash in his sock. "Stay busy out here, dude," he said to Anthony without looking at him. "All day, every day. Work for me an' you can make some paper. Enough so you can pay another nigga to go to the store for you."

Anthony laughed but shook his head. The bags were getting heavy, and he switched them around. "I'm straight," he said, and nodded good-bye to everyone there. "Need to get home, before my momma start trippin'."

Farther down the block he saw his big brothers, Darnell and Andre, slouched on the front stairs at John Mays's house, bobbing to beats that pumped through an open window. John stood on the porch above them, resting his ashy elbows on the banister while his quick tongue and fingers put the finishing touches on a blunt. Andre nodded and then scooted over. "Cop a squat, little nigga," he said. "What you get from the store?"

Instead of telling him, Anthony passed the bags and then sat down hard. Seconds later, Andre's hands were rooting around inside the plastic sacks while Darnell scowled at him.

"Anything sweet?"

"Yeah," Andre said, and tossed up the pads. "Chew on these."

"Chew these nuts," Darnell answered, and threw them back. "Ain't no cookies in there?" He looked at Anthony and the boy shook his head. Cookies hadn't been on the list.

"Got some Cheerios."

Darnell frowned and leaned back on his hands. "What I look like, eating some Cheerios?"

Weed smoke, thick and danky, rolled from John's mouth and churned in the open air before the wind bundled it up and took it away. "I got some cookies in the house," John offered. "Chocolate chip. They good as hell."

Anthony looked at Darnell, who was staring at Andre. The three of them shook their heads together and then laughed. "Cookies and roach eggs," Andre said. "You can keep that shit to yourself."

They laughed louder, except for John, who took savage pulls from the blunt. He inhaled and exhaled, inhaled and exhaled until the end was bright red. "Like yaw niggas ain't got roaches," he said finally, and more to himself. "Everybody around here got some bugs."

Darnell reached for the weed. "Other niggas got roaches, but them roaches got you. How much they be chargin' you for rent?"

More laughter, and this time even John joined in. There was no use in arguing with the obvious. In the house, the stereo played "To Live and Die in L.A." and all their heads bobbed knowingly, even though the closest any of them had ever been to Los Angeles was Detroit.

John looked at the three brothers and hit the blunt again. Then he passed it to the left and laughed out a cloud. "I was just noticing . . . all three of yaw got some big-ass heads!"

Even Darnell smiled a little. People said the Jones boys had heads built for football.

"Forget you, man," Andre said. "You know what they say about big-head niggas?"

"What? Yaw cain't buy no hats?"

"Big dicks," Andre said.

"Big brains," Darnell added matter-of-factly.

"Kiss my ass. Maybe Ant, down there," John said, aiming a narrow finger at the youngest. "Little dude goin' to college next year an' shit. What happened to yaw?"

"The same thing that happened to you, dumb nigga," Andre said. "East Cleveland Public Schools."

"I ain't goin' to no college," Anthony protested.

Darnell looked at him with disappointment or regret, but really, Anthony couldn't tell. His oldest brother's face was always a flatline. "College, boardin' school, you know what that fool saying."

"So? I still ain't going nowhere. They probably ain't even gon' let me in."

"You gon' get in," Darnell said confidently. "Schools like that be loving them some black people. Probably gon' throw you a basketball and some tap shoes as soon as you get there." He laughed, but it was hollow. Anthony didn't say anything else because he knew that he couldn't win.

In time, the song inside ended. When nothing else came on Darnell hawked and spat a brown blob. "Roaches cut your 'lectricity?"

John jumped from his perch and disappeared through the door. Seconds later, Jay-Z's latest bumped through the window and John came back, smiling. Someone sparked another blunt and they passed it around, but it never came to Anthony. It was time to get home; his mother would be worried. People had a way of getting robbed after dark.

When he got to the house, his mother yelled at him for taking so long and then disappeared into the bathroom. Left to himself, Anthony went to his room, plopped down on the bed, and scooped a book from the floor. It was *The Stand* by Stephen King. Inside, the characters tried to survive in a plague-stricken world while a dark man in cowboy boots and an old black woman fought for their souls. It was just the kind of stuff that Anthony liked to read; the kind of thing he even secretly hoped to write someday.

"You doing your homework?"

His mother's voice at the bottom of the stairs made him jump. "Yeah, Ma. I'm doing it right now." He dove for his bag and dumped it on the bed. Textbooks and boring math sheets covered the comforter. He got to work and then lost track of time. When he looked up again, it was full dark outside the window and cold gusts rattled the frames. He hated the season and the need for gloves, the black slush splashed up on his pants and coat by moving cars. Walks to Floyd's took twice as long and meant stinging cheeks and numbing toes, bitter breezes and awkward falls that made him want to curl up and quit. His middle school principal, Mr. Davis, had said that up in Maine it was winter nearly all year long. How did they expect him to live through that?

The phone rang and it was Floyd. He was in a car with Mookie and Curtis, and they were on their way over to pick him up. Anthony went downstairs to find his mother gone and Darnell in front of the television, eating Cheerios from a mixing bowl. Anthony started to say something smart but asked for five dollars instead. "Come on, I'll pay you back."

"How you gonna pay me back, little nigga?" Darnell asked. "You ain't got no job."

"I got five dollars somewhere upstairs. Soon as I find it, I'll hit you back."

Darnell slurped his cereal, stared at the TV, and grunted. Jerry Seinfeld and his crew were trying to figure out if a local store's yogurt truly was fat free. "I cain't get into that white boy humor," he said, and changed to BET. "What you need money for?"

"Why do it matter?" A horn sounded in the driveway. "Come on, man. Five dollars."

Darnell clacked his teeth on the spoon and winced, fished a five-dollar bill from his pocket. "You better pay me back, Ant. Don't think I'ma let you slide."

"I know." The bill disappeared quickly. "Soon as I got five, you got five."

Curtis's Buick was like a rolling massage. There was no spare tire, no jack, no road flare in his trunk of funk;

only the subwoofers, amps, and blinking lights he made sure to show all of his friends. One day, Anthony knew, Curtis was going to show it to one person too many and have no stereo or car to flaunt. But for now, everything was cool, and he was happy to be where he was, floating in a car full of people with music so loud it made talking a waste of time.

In front of the store, sipping wine and telling lies, were the gray and dusty men who gathered there every day, blowing into cupped hands and rocking on unsteady legs. Ant saw his father standing among them, a big and leathery hand choking the throat of a forty-ounce bottle of beer. His dad saw him, too. It was too late to turn around.

"Well, lookey here." Moses Jones opened his arms, but Anthony slapped his empty hand instead. "Too big for all that, huh? Not too big to knock out, though." His father threw a playful punch and Anthony dodged it, then he threw an anemic punch of his own.

The other men looked on while they boxed, Anthony embarrassed but trying not to show it. Floyd and Mookie exited the store carrying paper bags. They nodded to the fighters and got into the car.

Anthony dropped his hands. "Gotta go."

His father smiled at him. "You know I'm proud of you, right?"

Anthony looked away, but his old man was still in front of him, waiting for an answer.

"You don't wanna go, do you?" Moses said finally.

Anthony kicked a hole in the snow with his heel and sighed.

His father laughed. "It's awright. You only gotta do two things in this world: stay black and die. Everything else is up to you."

Anthony made a face and his father nodded knowingly. "Don't mind yo' momma," he said. "She be tryin' to act all big 'n' bad, but put yo' foot down. You'll see."

"Like you did?"

"That was different," Moses said after a pause. "Husband an' wife shit. Plus I messed that one up. You ain't got nuthin' to worry about as long as you ain't done nuthin' wrong."

"I guess so."

Quick as a blink, his father pulled him close. "See?" He chuckled. "The old man still got some speed left in him." They hugged quickly, patted each other on the back, and then separated.

"Good to see you," Anthony said.

"You, too."

"Tell yo' momma I said hi. And tell her I still ain't remarried." He winked and went back to his friends.

Inside the car, Anthony stared at the unopened bottle of Private Stock between his knees and thought about his father. He didn't remember living with him, although his mother said they stayed married until Anthony was four. What he did remember, though, were the broken promises; fishing trips that never happened because somebody had broken into his car and stolen the poles; birthday presents, mailed instead of hand delivered, that the post office always managed to lose. The lies were weak, but Anthony played them off. It was his father's way of saving face, and deep down he believed that his old man would do all of those things if he could, even if Anthony's mother thought the man was incapable of doing anything good at all.

Anthony leaned forward and tapped Curtis on the shoulder. "Yo, run me to the crib, man."

In his driveway, Ant nodded a quick good-bye to his

friends and slid his key into the deadbolt, but didn't open the door. People upstairs. Andre and Darnell, John Mays and some girls. He could hear them laughing and saw the twin living-room windows glowing red like demon eyes. "Fuck lights" was what Andre called the red bulbs he kept in the drawer along with his rubbers, his weed, and his X-rated movies. He only used them when they had girls over. And he only had girls over when they knew their mother would be gone overnight.

She had a new man, tall and light-skinned, with reddish-brown hair. He carried a briefcase and talked like a white boy, even though he looked a little like Malcolm X. His name was Patrick, and he hardly ever came into the house, opting instead to beep the horn from the safety of his locked Lexus. The man could go ahead and sleep with his mother, as far as Anthony was concerned. But he would never be his daddy.

His daddy.

Leaning against the back of the house now, Anthony briefly entertained thoughts of his parents together, living the TV sitcom life of sit-down meals, neighborly neighbors, help with homework, and warm hugs and kisses before restful nights. Anthony laughed, but nothing about it was funny.

Flakes, floating softly like ash, brushed Anthony's cheeks and turned to water. It was late and he had school tomorrow, despite the red lights in the windows. He would just have to sleep in his mother's room, since it was clear that she wouldn't be coming home.

TWO

ANTHONY SAT IN THE BACK ROW OF ENGLISH
class, eyes shut and listening to a recording of "The
Cask of Amontillado." Ms. Kennedy, their teacher,
was pretty and young, and she liked to wear low-cut
dresses. But she also exposed her students to Poe and
to Plath. Sometimes she even showed movies.

Half of the class had gone to sleep right away, while
some others cracked jokes or fidgeted. But Ant was
caught up, mesmerized and enthralled by the hollow
scrape of the spatula, the tombstone grate of brick
against brick as Montresor sealed Fortunato in the
cellar. "I wouldn'ta never went down there," he said
absently, and opened his eyes.

Next to him, his best friend lifted his head from the desk and shook it. "Hell naw," Floyd agreed. "Over some wine, nigga? Old dude must be crazy."

"Or a alcoholic." They snorted. Ms. Kennedy turned toward them and put a finger to her lips. Floyd stuck up a different finger but held it low, behind the desk.

"I got somethin' for her mouth," Floyd said. "Got somethin for that juicy booty, too."

Ms. Kennedy looked up angrily and shook her head. "Yeah," Floyd continued, more to himself than to his friend. "Bet she like one of them white teachers in the suburbs. Be boning her favorite students, on the low."

Ant sniffed and checked her out. She was grading papers, and her breasts rested heavy on the top of the desk. His mouth watered. "You probably right, playa," he said hopefully. "After school, she might be a freak."

"That's what's up," Floyd whispered, and the two of them bumped fists.

Just then, the door swung open and in walked Virgil Sheeley: hall monitor, student council president. Punk. He had a note but announced his news anyway. Anthony Jones was wanted in the principal's office.

"Damn, Ant," Floyd said as the rest of the class

murmured. "Davis be on yo' back, nigga. Whachoo do this time?"

Ant shrugged, shoved books into his bag, and flung one strap over his shoulder. "Where you gon' be after school?"

"We be somewhere," Floyd answered. "Probably the same spot as usual."

At the front of the room, Ms. Kennedy slapped her desk hard and hooked a thumb toward the door. "Get a move on, Mr. Jones. Right now."

"Yes, ma'am."

In the office, Mr. Davis was nestled in the broad chair that farted when he moved. It was in front of his desk, a few feet across from the little straight-backed vinyl job he kept for students. The rule was simple: behind his desk and sitting in the swivel, he was Mr. Davis the scowling principal who detained, suspended, or expelled. But in front of the desk he was the princi*PAL*, the good-natured buddy who liked to talk about sports and use ancient slang.

"Take a load off, brother man," he said, grinning. "Let's rap."

Ant fought the urge to roll his eyes and sat down across from his principal. For a while he watched the spinning ceiling fan. Then he looked at the framed picture of Davis and Mike Tyson on the wall, the shelves filled with statues and knickknacks instead of books, and at Mr. Davis, who was staring patiently at him with eyes doubly magnified by thick glasses. "So," the man said, and smacked his hands on his meaty neck. "You heard from that school yet?"

"No."

The principal reached for the phone. "When are they supposed to let you know? You want to call them?"

Anthony tried to protest, but it was too late. Stubby fingers were stabbing buttons. Soon Mr. Davis was talking to Mr. Kraft, the director of admissions at Belton. Their conversation was a verbal roller coaster, big fits of loud laughter followed by murmured words. Judging by his principal's body language, not only had Anthony been accepted, but he had also been given heavy financial aid.

The news confused and numbed him. He could feel Davis's big eyes boring in, waiting for him to say something, but what was he supposed to do? His whole life had been in East Cleveland. Did they really expect him to just walk away?

The principal moved to the familiar corner of his

desk and grinned. "Looks like a done deal," he said. "Our loss is Belton's gain. What's your mother's number at work?"

There was a long pause. Anthony let his head roll back and looked at the ceiling. Rising tears blurred his view but didn't fall. He wouldn't let them. It was a matter of pride and survival. Kids who cried got beat up all the time. "I'll tell her."

Anthony left the principal's office just before the final bell. Doors opened and lockers slammed as black kids streamed through the exits. He found Floyd and Mookie down the block, leaning on a building across the street from the police station. Then he took his place with them, against the wall.

"What he want?" Floyd asked, not bothering to look at him.

"Nuthin'." Ant slipped off his coat and wiped his brow with the heel of his hand. It came away slimy. "It's hot out here. You know, for March." He watched a group of approaching girls, Shameeka Lewis in front of the pack, talking loud and fast. Ant didn't like her because she told everybody he couldn't kiss. He could kiss just fine, though. He just hadn't liked kissing her.

She bumped him as she passed, deliberately and

hard. He could have let it go, but Ant decided not to. "Better watch out, ho."

The girls stopped at once and spun around. "What you call me?" Shameeka snapped.

Before Ant could say another word, Mookie nudged him aside and raised his hand. "Go on, girl, before you get slapped."

Shameeka looked at the hand and laughed. Floyd laughed, too, and so did the other girls. Mookie's face never changed, though, and Ant braced himself. He knew that his friend wouldn't think twice about hitting Shameeka, a grandmother, or anyone else.

"This fool done lost his mind," Shameeka said over her shoulder. "Better put that toy down, fool. You don't even know how to use it." She grabbed Mookie's arm, but he snatched it away.

"Do it again," he warned, and stuck a finger in her face. "Go on 'head and touch this toy, so I can show you how I play."

"Chill, Mook," Ant said almost desperately. "You fi'n to get in trouble over some nonsense."

"Better listen to your boy." She grabbed Mookie's finger, just as the bigger boy's other hand clapped the side of her head. A shining earring flew into the street, and

Shameeka slumped bonelessly to the ground.

"Told that bitch not to touch me." Mookie lifted his hand to take another swing, but Floyd said something before Anthony could.

"Don't do that shit," he said flatly. "Leave her alone."

Mookie lowered his hand without protest. Shameeka drew a big breath and wailed. One of her friends rushed over and bent to her aid. "You ain't hafta hit her like that," the girl said, lovingly brushing dirt from her face. "What kinda nigga is you, punching on girls?"

"A real nigga! What you think?"

Shameeka blinked at him from her place on the concrete. Her friends helped her to her feet and led her away, shouting threats over their shoulders.

Twenty minutes later, the boys were still on the corner. Mookie made a joke about how fast Shameeka had hit the ground, and when no one responded, he sulked. "She hit me first." He went into the street and grabbed the abandoned earring. "Here you go, Dr. Phil," he said, trying to hand it to Floyd. "Give it back and she might give you some stank."

Floyd smacked his hand and the hoop went tumbling again, this time landing in ragged bushes. Anthony stared at the earring and then back at his friends, who were squared off like they were ready to fight. He knew that they wouldn't, though. Mookie was bigger and had a bad rep, but Floyd was their leader. It had been that way since kindergarten.

"Both of yaw need to chill," Anthony said. "We don't need to be fighting each other."

Floyd started walking and Anthony fell into place by his side, with Mookie trailing close behind them. "Mr. Davis told me some shit today," Anthony said, and then immediately regretted opening his mouth.

"What?" Floyd said, not breaking stride. "Thought you said he ain't want nuthin'?"

"It was about that school . . . guess I got in."

Behind them, Mookie laughed, but the other two boys got quiet. Anthony suddenly wanted to be somewhere else. "The nigga Ant 'bout to hit reform school and ain't never been arrested," Mookie said. "Your moms be trippin' hard!"

"Just 'cause I got in don't mean I'm gon' go," Ant said, glowering. "Plus, it ain't no reform school, anyway. How many times I gotta tell you that?"

"About a million," Floyd said. "And even then, this dumb nigga still won't understand."

They reached the point where each boy went in a different direction. Anthony turned a corner and was surprised to see his mother's car squatting in their driveway.

Maxine Jones was an inch shorter than her youngest boy but every bit as strong. Muscles rippled her calves when she wore shorts or dresses, and they creased her angry arms. She ruled her boys like an overseer, snapping her belt and whipping them instead of using child psychology. But with age and growing size came a kind of emancipation; for his brothers the leather strap had already lost its sting. That day was coming for Anthony, and it was coming soon. He would welcome freedom from the belt, but it also made him sad. After him, she would have no one left to take care of.

He opened the door and went inside, found the house dark and still. His iron mother was in bed, home early with a stomach bug.

"Where you been, anyway?" she asked hoarsely. "School ended damn near two hours ago."

"I had detention . . . sorry."

She rolled her eyes toward him without moving her head. "Don't know how in the world you expect to go to that school if you cain't stop acting like a fool."

"What if I don't get in?" He sat on the edge of the mattress. "Would it be so bad if I had to stay here with you?"

"You'll get in," she said, not looking at him. "You as good as gone, I can feel it." She grabbed his hand then and rubbed it. "My baby gon' be the next president!" Her smile quickly faded and then disappeared altogether. She dropped his hand and looked at him sternly. "Now once you get up there, you cain't get in no trouble. No fights, no detentions, no nothing."

"I know, Ma. . . ."

"And make sure to be friends with them white people. Somebody's daddy might give you a job."

He swallowed hard. "But what if I don't wanna go? Do I get any say at all?"

"Of course you do," she answered. "As long as you do what I tell you, you can have all the say in the world." She laughed and turned the TV to Oprah. The audience was screaming over gifts.

The next night Anthony found himself at Reggie's house, playing video games with friends. By then, he had told his mother the Belton news and was tired of hearing her brag to her friends. It was good to spend some quality time with people who didn't care about Maine.

What they did care about, though, was beer. Anthony volunteered to go out and buy more, along with Mookie, who said he needed some air. They had tried to get Floyd to make the trip too, but he was busy kicking ass in John Madden football. It was dark outside and getting cooler. Mookie fumbled with his unzipped coat and mumbled drunken lyrics.

"Fuck a white cop at the end of my block, got the Glock in my sock and it's ready to pop, make that blood drip-drop on the ground like it's hot, till his fuckin' heart stop beating bullshit . . ."

Mookie stopped dead in his tracks and raised his arms like a heavyweight champion, obviously pleased with his latest freestyle. "Oh, shit. You hear that shit, nigga? Off the top of the dome, nigga. Now that's what's up."

"I heard. We gon' have to start calling you Fi'teen Cent."

"Forget you, man. Don't ask to be in the video."

They got to the store and bought two bottles of Olde

English. Back outside, they were halted by a disheveled man with a salt-and-pepper beard. "Hey, Johnny," the man said, stepping in front of them. "You got any spare change?"

"Hell naw," Mookie snapped. "Get a job."

"Johnny . . . ?"

Mookie kept walking, but Anthony stopped and gave the man all the change in his pockets. "Here you go, dude. It ain't much, but you might get a nip."

"God bless you, Johnny," the man said, and approached someone else.

The boys walked in silence for a while. Anthony could feel his friend looking at him, but he wouldn't look back. "Why you be givin' that nigga money all the time?" Mookie finally asked. "He don't even know yo' name. Johnny. Who the hell is Johnny?"

"Why you be askin' me the same question all the time?"

"How come you don't never answer?"

Anthony didn't say anything. Sometimes it was best to ignore him. They came to a brick-strewn and muddy lot with a low fence. "Let's cut through," Anthony said. "I need to hurry up and hit the bathroom."

"Pee right here. Ain't nobody looking at you."

Anthony made a face. "I ain't gotta pee, dawg."

Mookie nodded, but he still kept to the sidewalk. "Naw man, you can make it. It be big-ass rats in there at night."

Anthony pleaded, but Mookie shook his head and moved more deliberately. They were halfway to the corner, anyway. Just then, a blue Buick pulled to the curb. A light-skinned man in the passenger seat stared hard at them through his sunglasses. Anthony wanted to dash, but another fear gripped him. If he wound up running for no good reason, the teasing would be merciless.

"Yo, cuz," the passenger said, leaning out the open window. "Yaw know where we can cop some weed at?"

Anthony stayed where he was but his friend moved closer. "Back that way," Mookie said pointing. "Past the RTA station. Niggas always be there."

The boys continued walking toward the corner, not saying anything. Anthony wanted to turn around and look but kept stopping himself. He was afraid though. Something felt wrong. Weed was everywhere in East Cleveland, and the dope spots were obvious. The men were either cops or something worse. Anthony checked over his shoulder and then didn't care about getting teased. The car was trailing quietly behind them, close to the curb. "We gotta cut through."

Mookie looked and his eyes got wide, but he sniffed and stuck to the sidewalk. "You cut through, nigga," he said. "I ain't no punk."

A sound from the street made Anthony turn again. The passenger was out of the car and moving toward them, his head on a swivel and right arm glued to his thigh.

"RUN!" Ant threw the beer in the air and vaulted the fence. His feet stumbled over things that he couldn't see, but he kept going. The man shouted, and then there were two quick explosions. Something angry whistled past Anthony's ear, and he dropped face-first in the mud. He wanted to cry and to run and to pray; he wanted to crawl to safety. But he was too petrified to move, too scared to stop the spreading warmth in his crotch.

Ant stayed still and listened long for more gunshots or footsteps. What had the man shouted? Was it gangs or money? Shameeka or something else? Slowly he rolled over onto his back and lifted his muddy head. The Buick was nowhere in sight. But neither was his friend.

"Mookie?"

He called him again, more urgently. "Mookie-Mook? Where you at, man? I think they gone." Still no answer. He hoped that his friend had run away, but somehow Anthony didn't believe it.

He got to his knees and saw a dark bulk on the fence, knew that it was Mookie, and ran over. His friend was bent over the top rail at the waist, dripping blood. Bits of brain were in his hair and on the ground like chewed bubblegum.

Anthony ran to the store and begged for help, went back to his friend and stood guard but tried not to look at him. Soon there were sirens and people with badges who asked him all kinds of questions. No, he and Mookie were not in a gang and no, neither one of them sold drugs. He gave a description of the man and the car but hadn't thought to look at the license plate.

An ambulance came and then more policemen. They set up lights and unrolled yellow tape to control the growing crowd. After that, the television trucks arrived and parked halfway on the sidewalk. White reporters in expensive clothes stood in front of scruffy cameramen, stared grimly into living rooms, and shared the latest news: Another kid had been gunned down in East Cleveland.

And all the while as they talked, Mookie stayed bent over the fence, away from the cameras but bleached by other floodlights. Police and detectives scuttled around him like crabs, sometimes laughing. Why did they have to go for more beer? Why did Mookie slap Shameeka like that? Why had Mookie been too proud to run?

An officer, the first one Anthony had talked to, came over and leaned into the open cruiser. "How you doing, there, kid? Just a few more minutes and we can take you home."

"It ain't right for him to still be up there like that," Anthony said. "Somebody need to take him down."

The officer held up his hand. "Wait a second, they will. We just have to finish the initial investigation. . . . It sure would be nice if you could remember something else. If not the license plate, a motive? Anything?"

"What about a sheet? Cain't you at least cover him up?"

The officer started to say something but closed his mouth. Then he went and found an EMT. Minutes later, someone brought a sheet and draped it over the body. The officer came back. "So, you ready to go?"

"Don't worry about it. I'll walk." Ant stood up and started off. He went in the wrong direction at first but crossed the street and doubled back. His feet were heavy and numb. It took a lot to pick them up and put them down. Mookie was dead and hanging over a fence; his brains were stuck in his hair. He would never get a record deal, never get to drive a car or live on his own. He was fourteen years old and done with his life, while Anthony was walking home. It didn't feel right.

Before long, Ant stood on his porch but didn't go through the door. The red lights were on in the windows upstairs, and he could hear loud music and laughter. He sat on the steps and stared at the lawn, wanted to be alone but needed company.

He started walking again. It was dark and too cold for the clothes he was wearing, but Anthony didn't care very much about comfort. He didn't care about the drying mud on his pants, and he didn't care about his damp crotch, either. He just walked with his chin on his chest and no destination in mind, walked because it was better than sitting. And it wasn't until he found himself in front of Mookie's house that Anthony realized he'd walked too far.

There were people standing outside under the porch light, Mookie's mother crying inside of a circle of women, her other sons looking angry and helpless. More people were scattered around the little yard, including Floyd and other eighth graders. Anthony thought about turning around, but his best friend saw him before he could move.

"Ant!" Floyd rushed over with a couple of other boys close behind him. All of their faces were strained. "What the hell? What happened?"

Ant told them about the car and the thin man in sunglasses, about the gunshots and Mookie hanging over the fence. And he told them about the police and the TV reporters, how none of them really seemed to care very much about their friend.

"Like that's a surprise," Floyd said woodenly. "Mook wasn't no white boy from Pepper Pike."

Just then Paulette, Mookie's older sister, came rushing off the porch, shoeless and in a bathrobe. She ran directly to Anthony and clung to his arm. "It wasn't him, right?" she pleaded. "Mookie ain't dead, Ant. Say they lying!"

Anthony opened his mouth and closed it, shook his head, and then Paulette collapsed on the sidewalk. Caring hands carried her back into the house. Ant followed them and stopped on the porch, in front of

Mookie's numb mother. "I'm sorry," he croaked. "We tried to run but . . . I don't know . . . we tried. I'm sorry."

She opened her arms and pulled him in. "I know," she said. "I know, baby. He loved you. You know that, don't you? He loved all of you boys just like you was his brothers."

"We loved him, too." They held each other a while longer, and then, without a word, Anthony turned around and walked home.

It took a lot of banging, but Andre finally answered the door. He laughed when he saw his little brother. "Momma gon' beat that ass for messing up your school clothes," he said. "And she gon' beat it again for losing your key."

"Mookie got shot." Anthony said plainly. "He dead." He pushed past his gawking brother and stopped, could hear Darnell and other people upstairs, could smell the weed smoke and wine. He wanted to go and yell in their faces, he wanted respect for the dead. But Anthony was tired and his feet wouldn't move, so he stabbed the button on the remote and let Letterman into the living room.

"You for real?"

"Wish I wasn't." His eyes were locked on the screen. They burned, but he didn't blink.

Andre nudged him. "What happened?"

Anthony stoically recounted the story. When he finished, his brother left the room and came back with a bottle, "Sorry, man," Andre said. "That's some messed-up shit for a little kid to be dealing with."

Anthony shrugged and twisted the beer cap. "I ain't no little kid," he said, and took a long drink. Then he thought about Maine and endless winter. White world or not, it had to be better than East Cleveland. It had to be better than what happened to Mookie. "I ain't no little kid," Anthony repeated, more for himself than his brother. "And I ain't staying here no more."

THREE

THAT SUMMER, ANTHONY STILL HUNG OUT WITH
his friends, but almost never at night. They talked
about Mookie but less and less, until his name hardly
came up at all. They still got quiet when they passed
his house, or when they saw any of his family on the
street. It wasn't that they had forgotten about their
friend. It just hurt too much to talk about him.

Floyd was busy anyway, selling weed for Shane.
And Anthony got an unofficial job in Shaker Heights,
sweeping hair at a barbershop. He rode his bike up the
hill every day, past the wide lawns and white people.
All his life they had been foreign to him, living close by
but in a different world. That would change, though,

once he got to Maine. More than likely, his roommate would be some billionaire from Beverly Hills.

He was excited but scared, too. And on the morning that he was supposed to leave, Anthony lay awake in the predawn darkness, fighting panic. What if his first plane ride turned out to be his last? There were terrorists and sometimes the engines fell off. What if he got to school and couldn't handle the work? Would they put him in special ed or just send him back home? Maybe he should have listened to Floyd and refused to go.

He looked at his sleeping brothers and felt jealous. They pretty much knew what their day would bring. But for Anthony, it would be a plane ride to Boston and then another to Portland, Maine. After that, Belton Academy and the unknown.

An hour later, at a rare breakfast together, Anthony joked with his brothers and mother about Maine. Andre made a crack about igloos and Eskimos, but Darnell corrected his geography. Their mother seemed happy and, simultaneously, sad. She laughed out loud sometimes but never for very long.

"I want you to be good when you go up there," she said. "Ain't nobody in this family never had a chance like this. Maybe you can even go to a four-year university." She beamed at the thought of it, and Anthony cringed. Not a single male branch of their family tree had even applied to college.

"I'll be good," he said while his big brothers grinned. "Just hope I can make some friends."

"Don't even worry about that," Darnell added confidently. "Do like I told you and everything gon' be straight."

"I will."

"And don't go up there and get none of them white girls pregnant, neither."

"Andre!"

"You don't have to worry about that, Ma," Anthony said. "I'm gon' go up there and keep to myself. Make no trouble, make no waves." He looked at his oldest brother, who was nodding appreciatively. "I ain't even gon' speak to nobody unless they speak to me first."

"Don't you go up there with no attitude. You need to leave all that nonsense right out there in those streets. . . ."

"I know, Ma."

". . . All your little ghetto friends and their ghetto ways, you know how easy it could have been you and not that Mookie boy?"

"I know, Ma. . . . I know."

The fierceness drained from her eyes and was replaced by relief. "Well, hurry up and get your things together," she said. "You don't wanna miss your flight." She stood stiffly and started collecting dishes. Anthony moved his bags to the front door and then picked up the phone. It was early, but he had promised to call before he left.

"Wake up, man," Anthony joked when his best friend answered. "Still got time to catch that flight."

"Go on with that garbage," Floyd said sleepily. "So, is you ready?"

"I guess so."

Floyd sniffed. "Don't guess, nigga. Either you ready or you ain't."

"I know, man. It's just . . . I don't know." Silence, except for the sound of his best friend's breathing. Anthony wanted to say more but didn't know how. "I'll be back home in like two months, anyway. You know, for Thanksgiving."

"That's what's up. . . . Ain't that where your boy from, anyway? Stephen King?"

Anthony thought before saying anything. As far as

he could remember, they had never talked about his favorite author. "How did you know that?"

"Because I pay attention, nigga," Floyd said. "Just like I know you be writing your own stories sometimes. You ain't never showed me one, but I know, anyway."

"Damn. You like a teenage detective."

Floyd laughed. "Wrong side, playa. If you ever write about me, make me a criminal who don't never get caught."

Someone tapped Anthony's shoulder. It was his oldest brother, and he was holding the biggest bag. "Hurry up, fool," Darnell said, heading toward the front door. "Momma already waiting."

"I gotta go," Anthony said.

"Awright, man. I'll holler. And rep E.C., nigga!" Floyd blurted. "Don't forget where you from."

"I won't."

He hung up, took a last look around the house, and then went down the front stairs. His brothers stood quietly outside of the car, both of them looking stunned. Anthony understood. But just like it had been on the phone with Floyd, his mouth couldn't find the words.

At the airport, his mother cried, but Anthony wouldn't. He had to show that he could be a man. She made him promise to be good and study hard, made him swear that he wouldn't do anything stupid. "Do it right," she said earnestly, and squeezed him one last time. "Show those people that you belong."

"I will," he said, and let her go. "I promise."

The plane touched down in Portland, and Anthony took a deep breath. The whole day he'd been afraid of a crash, but now he was afraid that he'd made it. He was in Maine, impossibly far from everyone that he knew. If there was trouble, he would have to handle it alone.

He followed the crowd off the plane and to the baggage claim area. They talked to one another or into cell phones as they waited for their luggage. Anthony wished that he had a phone, but his mother wouldn't buy him one. And every penny he'd made that summer had gone toward school.

He found his bags and went outside, looked around for a limousine but found a big van instead. It was dark blue, with BELTON ACADEMY printed on the sides. A bearded man in a flannel shirt and blue jeans leaned against it, reading a newspaper and moving his lips. He was the kind of white man that Anthony had seen a hundred times: in the hardscrabble neighborhoods on the near west side; pissed off and full of beer after Browns games, looking for a fight. They were dangerous and always seemed to hate black people. Anthony wondered if he had made a big mistake.

The man looked up and smiled at him. Then he folded his newspaper and started across the road.

"Anthony Jones?"

"Yeah."

"Hey, Tony. John Dunlap. I work maintenance over at the academy."

"Call me Ant."

They shook hands, and Anthony followed him to the back of the van, where John swung the doors open. Someone else was inside. Anthony could see skinny legs.

"Ant, huh?" John continued as he loaded the first bag. "Like the bug? Ever go by Tony? You know, like Tony Soprano?"

"Naw."

The man grabbed the other piece of luggage and sized him up. "That's okay," he said with a laugh. "I guess nobody's gonna take you for Italian, anyway."

Anthony climbed into the van and saw the other

passenger; a pale white girl with braces and dark hair. "Hi," she said, smiling desperately. "My name's Alison, what's yours?"

"Anthony Jones."

The girl giggled and extended her hand. "Hello, Mr. Jones."

They left the airport and drove onto a modest highway, Alison leaning on the back of Anthony's seat and talking nonstop. She was in the ninth grade, just like him, and from a town in Connecticut, not far from New York. Before Belton, she had been in a private middle school, and her biggest hope was to make the varsity ski team.

"What about you?" she asked. "Do you ski?"

He shook his head. "Never even seen a ski before."

"Oh."

They came up on a hitchhiker but blew right by her. The lonely scene made Anthony think of horror stories. He leaned forward and tapped the driver's shoulder. "Stephen King live around here?"

"Not here," John answered. "Up in Bangor. I hear he's one crazy bastard."

They turned onto another road, where trees pressed in like an advancing army. The lane wound past dilapidated farms and occasional houses.

"How much longer?"

John eyed him in the rearview. "Depends on the traffic. We may not have it like you New York boys, but you get caught behind some logging truck or some old fart and it'll feel like it."

"I ain't from New York," Anthony said. "I'm from East Cleveland."

"Cleveland," Alison said dreamily. "Did you ever meet LeBron James? You know, before he left?"

"Naw. He can eat a dick."

Color came to her cheeks, and her mouth flashed metal. "Wow. I really like the way you talk. Where I'm from, everyone sounds the same."

"Surprise, surprise." He saw Alison's wounded eyes and then looked out the window. He hadn't meant to hurt her, but at least she wasn't talking anymore.

They drove on, and Anthony didn't know he'd been sleeping, but John woke him with the horn. "Wakey-wake now, kiddies," the man announced. "You don't want to miss it."

Downtown Hoover was four blocks of stores and little restaurants, a firehouse, and a bank near the end of Main Street. There weren't any stoplights or bus shelters. There weren't any billboards or liquor stores. They drove up a hill and around a bend, past a neatly cut field, and then onto the divided campus, with buildings on both sides of the road. They parked in front of a brick building with white windows and green shutters. The sign above the entrance said KASTER HALL.

An acid bubble rose in Anthony's throat.

"Something else, ain't it?" John said from behind him. "Not a care in the friggin' world."

Anthony nodded but felt uneasy. Wasn't John part of that world, too? "Is this where I'm staying?"

"More than likely," John said. "Freshmen and sophomore boys in Kaster, juniors and seniors over there, in Welch." He chuckled and pointed to another dorm, across the street. "Try not to go in there by yourself."

"Why not?"

"Aww, you know upperclassmen," John said, still grinning. "Sometimes they like to horse around."

"Thanks." Anthony grabbed for his bags, but the man blocked him.

"Can't go in yet," John said, and pointed to a big building with white pillars. "You need to register first."

"Oh." He reached for his luggage, but John stopped him again.

"No need to lug everything up there."

Anthony hesitated. "Man, this is all I got."

John smiled patiently. "What part of the city you from? Brooklyn?"

"East Cleveland. Remember?"

"No fooling?" John scratched his head and looked him up and down again. "Well, this isn't Ohio, kid. Your stuff is safe."

Anthony went to the main building and registered. They gave him a lot of things to read plus his room key. John had been right: He was staying in Kaster Hall, on the freshman floor. He left the desk and moved through the crowded lobby, making sure not to bump anyone or even make eye contact. Most of the kids were with their parents, and all of them were white. Self-conscious, Anthony walked quickly toward the door. A man in a bow tie stopped him, though, before he could leave.

"Anthony Jones?"

Ant nodded but didn't say anything.

"Fantastic!" The man grabbed Anthony's hand and

shook it. "Good to meet you, Tony," he continued. "I'm Mr. Kraft, director of admissions."

"Nice to meet you, sir," Anthony said. "Thanks for letting me in."

"Nonsense. We should thank *you* for coming." Mr. Kraft clapped him on the shoulder and squeezed. Then he waved to a passing man in the crowd. He was big and had bushy eyebrows. "Tony, this is Mr. Rockwell. Coach, meet Tony Jones."

The tall man shook Anthony's hand and nearly broke it. "Welcome to Belton, Tony. Where you from?"

"Cleveland."

"Cleveland?" He made a face, and both of the men smiled. Anthony smiled, too, although he didn't know what was funny. "Had a kid here from Cleveland once, he could jump out the gym." The coach looked Anthony up and down. "What about you, Tony? You play any hoops?"

"Basketball?" Anthony thought about his brother's warning and shook his head. Didn't they see how short he was? "I ain't no good."

"Maybe not yet," Mr. Kraft said with a wink. "But give it time." The men shook Anthony's hand again and went off to talk together. Anthony returned across campus to his waiting bags and took them inside the dorm.

A boy named Zach greeted him and grabbed a suitcase. He was older and said he was a proctor. "So," he said, walking quickly. "Where you from?"

"Cleveland."

"Oh," the beefy boy said, and raised his eyebrows. "Figured you were from New York, like Big George and everybody else."

"Big who?"

Zach laughed. "George Fuller. You'll meet him. He pretty much owns this place." They came to a door at the end of the hall and stopped. "Here it is," Zach said. "Number four." Three people were already inside, a white man and woman, plus a boy in beat-up jeans. Zach cleared his throat loudly, but the family was already gawking. "Meet Anthony Jones," Zach said, and put the bag on the floor. "He'll be bunking here, with Brody."

The boy in jeans put down a box and came over. The name on his faded bowling shirt said GUS, even though Zach had just called him Brody. "So you're Tony Jones?" the boy asked, and glanced at his parents, who watched coolly from the far end of the room.

"Anthony," he corrected. "Or you can just call me Ant."

"Sweet!" the boy said, and shook Anthony's hand. "Brody Lavallee. Nice to meet you."

"You too."

The boy waved a hand between his parents and Anthony. "This is my mom and dad. Mom and Dad, Tony Jones." Mrs. Lavallee said hello from her spot near the wall, while her husband came off of it and shook Anthony's hand.

"That's *Jones*, right?" the grinning man asked suspiciously. "Not Jones Al-Salami?" The adults laughed. Brody jerked his head and glared at them.

Anthony stammered. Had they just called him a terrorist?

"He's just joking," Mrs. Lavallee said. "He's not very funny, but I think we'll keep him anyway."

Across the room, there was a guitar case leaning against a wall. Brody picked it up and brought it over. "You play?"

"Me?" Anthony said looking at it. "Naw, man. Not even close."

"Don't speak so soon, dude." Brody looked at his parents, who were unpacking things and speaking softly to each other. "Besides, I might have more in here to play with than just a guitar." He pinched his thumb and forefinger together, took an invisible puff, and sang, *"Inspirational inhalations . . . for my musical occupation."*

Brody laughed, but Anthony shook his head. It was the worst voice he had ever heard.

There was a brief meeting that night in the auditorium, where the headmaster, Dr. Dirk, explained way too many rules. All of the Belton freshmen were there, along with a handful of teachers. Anthony checked out their faces. Aside from a few Asians and one kid who looked Indian, he was adrift in a Caucasian sea.

And then he heard it. Someone laughed from the corner of the room. It sounded familiar to Anthony, like school assemblies at MLK. When his eyes adjusted and he saw the two black kids, he felt like yelling out. On stage, the headmaster reminded them of the freshman camping trip. Then he dismissed them to their dorms.

Anthony found the two boys. The tall one was Paul and the chubby one was Khalik. Both of them were from Brooklyn, but they had only met that morning. Paul seemed cool, but Anthony wasn't so sure about

Khalik. He talked too fast and never looked Anthony in the eye.

Inside the dorm, there was another meeting, this time with Mr. Hawley, an English teacher who was in charge of their floor. The man smiled a lot but also laid down the law, sometimes reading directly from the student handbook. The boys had cleaning jobs that rotated every Sunday. Plus they had morning room inspections and supervised study hall every weeknight. There were rules about bedtime and when to be awake; girls weren't allowed to visit their rooms, except for supervised occasions; and no one could leave campus before signing out with Mr. Hawley or another adult first. So much for all the prep school freedom Anthony had imagined. The regulations made him miss his mother's grocery lists.

An hour later he was lying in the dark and staring at the ceiling while his roommate slept soundly in the bunk underneath. Anthony suspected that the other boys on the floor were sleeping, too, but he couldn't keep his eyes closed. How far had he traveled in just one day?

Someone had put BELTON SUCKS in glow-in-the-dark letters on the ceiling, along with a bunch of little stick-on stars that formed an obscene constellation. It was supposed to be funny, but the cosmic blow job only made Anthony uncomfortable. He peered outside, but everything was pitch black. There weren't any streetlights, and no passing cars. He had never felt so out of place.

The next morning, Anthony and the rest of the freshmen left school for three days of camping. They brought equipment and canoes to a town called Rangeley, where there was a huge lake with islands. Anthony stood at the shore and watched the wide water, the sharp rocks beneath the surface, and the dented boats knocking together. He had never been camping or canoeing before and was starting to have second thoughts. He looked at Brody, who stood next to him, along with a short kid named Nate. "I don't know about this, man," Anthony said as the first few kids paddled off.

"Relax," Brody whispered. "These things are like impossible to sink."

"Unless you do it on purpose," Nate added, and laughed. He had already put shaving cream on everyone's doorknobs that morning, and the night before, he had run up and down the hallway, flapping his arms and squawking.

Anthony tapped the shorter boy's shoulder and whispered, "Do some dumb shit, if you want to. Hear?"

Nate stiffened and then turned around. "I was just joking."

In front of them, Brody took off his shoes and walked the canoe into the water. "Both you dudes need to chillax," he said. "The day is young, the sun is bright, and so are we. . . . Now get in the boat."

By the time they were a hundred feet from the shore, Anthony loosened his grip on the sides. He was in the middle seat, surrounded by gear and doing nothing, while the other two boys rowed easily. There was laughter and shouting from the rest of the boats. Some of the girls had stripped down to bikini tops, and a few of the boys were shirtless. Most of the canoes moved along in straight lines, but some of them hopelessly zigzagged. Anthony glanced at the third oar lying flat at his feet, picked it up, and dipped it into the lake.

"Way to go, dude!" Brody shouted. "Now let's blow the rest of these boats away!"

"That's what's up."

They dug in and Anthony rowed hard, leaving deep

swirls in the water. They reached the first island before everyone else, and Brody pulled something from his pocket. "A little herbal blessing before lunch?"

Anthony looked at the pipe in his roommate's hand, at the blobs on the lake that were his teachers and class-mates, approaching but still far off. He could get high and no one else would know it. Then again, he could get paranoid, fall out of the boat, and drown. There was no telling what kind of weed Brody was smok-ing. "Go on," Anthony said, still watching the other canoes. "I'll keep a lookout."

"Sweet!" Brody and Nate crashed off into the woods, while Anthony skipped flat rocks on the water.

After lunch, they rowed closer to the group, partly because they didn't know where they were going next but mostly because a teacher had yelled at them. There was talking and teasing between the boats, and a few kids used their paddles to slap water at one another. Anthony didn't take part in any of the horse-play, though. And he wouldn't let Nate and Brody do it, either. His clothes were new and he didn't want to get them wet.

They reached the final island, and Mr. Hawley and

the other teachers got the kids to work. Soon the entire camp was set up and Anthony relaxed in the mouth of his tent, watching everything. Nate squirted girls with a water bottle, Brody and a hippie girl named Venus slipped into the woods, and the Brooklyn boys traded big-city stories in front of a wide-eyed audience.

"Tired?"

Anthony looked up to see Ms. Atwood smiling down at him. She was young and pretty but way too nosy. It was the third or fourth time that day that she'd ambushed him with a question. "I'm straight," he said.

"Excuse me?"

"I mean, I'm okay. I'm not tired."

"Oh." Still grinning, she sat down close to him. "Well, that makes one of us. I'll sleep like a log tonight." She laughed and looked at Anthony, clearly hoping that he would laugh, too. He didn't, though, and eventually she put a hand on his arm. "What's the matter? Are you homesick?"

"No."

"Are you lonely?" She glanced at Paul and Khalik holding court, and then back at Anthony. "Those guys seem pretty fun. Have you met them yet?"

"I met 'em. They're straight."

"Oh," she said, lighting up. "Are they from the same part of the city as you?"

Anthony looked at her, shook his head, and then frowned. Did they think that every black person in the world came from New York? "I'm from Cleveland, Ms. Atwood. I wish people around here would get that right."

She shifted uncomfortably, and blood rushed to her face. Anthony was glad that she was embarrassed. "That was a dumb assumption," she said sincerely. "It'll never happen again, Tony. I promise."

Anthony rolled his eyes and caught movement at the edge of the woods. Brody came out, smiling wide and weaving between the trees. Venus emerged a few seconds later and teetered over to a group of girls. Anthony sighed. Maybe he should have smoked up when he had the chance.

"Don't worry," Ms. Atwood said, rubbing his arm again. "Making friends takes time."

He drew a breath but then let out the air. Telling the truth wouldn't get her off his back. "I'm making plenty of friends, Ms. Atwood," he said. "For real. Everything's fine."

She stared at him awhile and then smiled. "You mean

straight, right? Everything's straight?"

"Yeah, Ms. Atwood," Anthony said, grinning. "Straight as a gate."

After dinner, Khalik started telling more New York stories. Most of them were violent and filled with blazing guns. The tales sounded fake to Anthony, or at least exaggerated. He could tell that Paul smelled the bullshit, too, by the way that the other Brooklyn kid kept frowning.

"I got a story," Anthony said before he could stop himself. Everyone looked, and he suddenly felt hot.

"He talks?" one of the other kids said, and a few of them laughed. Anthony said to forget about it, but then they all urged him on.

"Okay," he said, and then swallowed. At first he was going to tell them about Mookie, but he changed his mind. He wasn't ready to share that story yet, especially with a bunch of rich white kids.

"There was this old dude who used to live on my street," he said. "Mr. McKinley. And he was mean as shit. He used to sit upstairs on his porch all day and yell at anybody who came near his grass. But these girls, Delores and Darnetta, lived in the downstairs half of the house, and we used to sit on their porch and play Uno." A few people nodded at the mention of the card game. It helped Anthony relax. "So one day we were down there, playing; me, the two sisters, my friend Floyd, and this dude named T-Bone. Mr. McKinley started yelling at us, but we mostly ignored him. Old dude got quiet after a while and we kinda forgot he was up there. Then all this water came down on top of T-Bone and he started screaming. We all jumped out the way and saw Mr. McKinley standing up there with a big pot in his hands, laughing his ass off."

"Oh my God," someone said from the other side of the fire. "He poured hot water on him? Is that true?"

Anthony nodded, feeling a twisted sense of civic pride. Brooklyn and Khalik could kiss his ass. "T-Bone went and told his big brother, Junebug," Anthony continued. "Bug was just outta jail and already crazy. Later on that night, he broke into Mr. McKinley's house and straight killed him. Cut him up in the bathtub . . ."

"Oh my God."

"But that ain't the scary part," Anthony said. "This happened when I was in the third grade, and ain't nobody lived in that house ever since. But somehow the front grass always stay cut, and if you go sit on the steps by yourself, drops of hot water come down on your head. . . ."

At first there was silence and Anthony wished he hadn't said anything. But then came the grins and questions.

"Cut him to pieces?"

"Did the police ever catch him?"

"To *pieces*?"

"Is that really a true story?"

"As true as I'm sitting here right now," Anthony said, even though he had lied about part of it. Mr. McKinley, the hot water, and the murder were real, but the house was only empty, not haunted. They didn't have to know that, though. It was better for them to believe in the angry spirit protecting his lawn, and that T-Bone's brother was still walking around somewhere, with his razor.

FOUR

THEY GOT BACK TO CAMPUS AFTER THE CAMPING trip and found it full of upperclassmen. Most of the ninth graders lingered outside to try to meet the older kids, but Anthony went straight to the bathroom. For days he had flatly refused to squat in the woods and he was just about ready to bust. Inside the stall, he saw that someone had scratched BELTON DIPLOMAS just above the roll. Next to that was a poem about a man from Nantucket, plus a few faded names and crude cartoons. Anthony smiled at a few of them and shook his head at others. He would get a Magic Marker and add to the wall, just as soon as he had something to say.

When he was done, he took a shower and then went back to an empty room. From upstairs came the sounds of doors opening and closing, of loud music and sophomores talking and laughing. How many of them came from houses with swimming pools? How many had butlers and their own bank accounts? Probably all of them. And they would all grow up to one day take their parents' places, running the world and ruining it for poor people.

He was hungry, and Anthony realized that lunch was nearly over. He got dressed and joined Paul and Khalik in the dining hall. They ate in front of the big windows and looked out for black faces, but didn't find any. The New York boys started talking about basketball, about Brooklyn neighborhoods and a dozen other things Anthony didn't know. And they called each other "son" and "kid" all the time, especially when they got excited.

Another black boy walked into the room, and Anthony got excited. He was tall and light-skinned, with an out-of-control afro. Not the kind of kid Anthony thought would come from New York. Maybe he was from Cleveland? Or at least someplace where they didn't call pop "soda."

Anthony said, "W'sup," to the approaching boy and made room at the table. But instead of sitting down or even nodding, the kid walked right by and joined two blond girls. They called him Claude and welcomed him with hugs and kisses.

"You see that?" Anthony turned to his classmates, but they were too busy arguing over basketball.

"Word, son," Khalik continued. "I been to the Rucker like every year, since it started."

Paul made a face. "Then you must be like a hundred years old."

Without a word, Anthony gathered his dishes and left. Paul and Khalik didn't seem to notice.

On his way to the dorm, Anthony ran into Zach and a bunch of other boys. They were standing in a circle and tossing a little bag in the air with their feet. "Tony Ohio," Zach said, kicking the bag across the circle. "How's it hanging?"

It made him mad, but Anthony tried not to show it. His proctor knew that he didn't like the name. "I'm straight," he said, walking backward. "And it's Ant, not Tony, man. You know that."

"Sorry, dude," Zach said in a way that made the older boys laugh. Then he kicked the bag to Anthony, where it rolled to a stop at his feet. "Wanna hack?"

"Naw, man, some other time. I gotta go make a phone call."

"Yeah, *man*," said a big kid with a ponytail. "We'll catch you some other time."

Back in his room, Anthony grabbed the roll of quarters that was meant for his laundry and went to the pay phone down the hall. There was one on every floor of every dormitory because it was hard to get cell phone reception in that mountainous part of Maine.

Darnell answered on the first ring, sounding tired and energized at the same time. All of the excitement left him, though, when he heard Anthony's voice. "I thought you was somebody else," he said sleepily. "W'sup, man? How all them white people treating you?"

"I hate this place," Anthony blurted. "Don't even get me started."

Darnell laughed. "I tried to tell you, little nigga, but you ain't wanna listen."

"I listened. I just didn't believe it would be this bad." Anthony told his brother about all the rules in the dorms and how everyone assumed he was from New York. When he shared what had happened with Mr.

Kraft and Coach Rockwell, Darnell laughed until he wheezed.

Anthony waited for the fit to die down and then said, "I'm serious, man. Put Momma on the phone. I ain't got no friends up here."

Just then, Nate walked by and slapped Anthony on the back. "Hi, Mom!" he shouted. "Send cookies!"

Darnell laughed again. "I though you ain't have no friends?"

"I don't. That dude is just crazy, he don't count. Serious, man, lemme talk to Momma."

"She ain't here," Darnell said. "To tell the truth, since you left, she ain't really been home at all."

That night Brody tossed and turned in his bed, blew his nose like a trumpet, and dropped the used tissues on the floor. Anthony was already awake and on edge. He wanted to jump down and punch his roommate for being so disgusting. Rich white kids should know better than to throw snotty rags all over the floor. Then again, maybe there was someone at home that Brody paid to pick his boogers. For time and a half, maybe they even wiped his ass, too.

"What's so funny?" Brody asked from his bunk. Until

then, Anthony hadn't realized he'd been laughing.

"You," Anthony snapped. "You have to be the one of the nastiest people in the world. Seriously, man. How hard would it be to throw those things in the garbage?"

Brody turned on a light and saw his mess. "Sorry, dude," he said, and then started cleaning up. When he was done, he reached for his guitar case.

"I know you ain't about to smoke in here," Anthony warned. "Take that shit to the bathroom or something."

Brody laughed and opened the case anyway. Instead of his pipe and weed, he produced the guitar instead. He strummed a few notes, and the sound was good. It was also way past midnight, though, and they were supposed to be asleep.

"Put that junk down, man," Anthony said. "You gon' mess around and get me in trouble."

"They can't hear us, dude," Brody said. Then he strummed the guitar again, but more softly than before. *"They can't hear us . . . but they fear us . . . put your trust in old Gus . . . and don't be so ser-i-ous . . ."* He ended the short song with a flourish and a triumphant *"Dude!"* Brody grinned and jerked his head aside to get the hair from his eyes. "Just made that up," he said.

"What do you think?"

Unsure of what to say, Anthony didn't say anything. He kind of liked the acoustic ditty, but he also wanted to throw the guitar out the window. It was almost like Brody was trying to be annoying. "You must wanna get your ass kicked," Anthony said finally.

"What?" Brody asked, sounding genuinely shocked. "What did I do?"

As if to answer, someone knocked sharply on the door.

"What's going on in there?"

It was Zach, and he sounded mad. Anthony shook his head. If he got in trouble over Brody's stupidity, then he really would punch him.

Zach knocked again and then pushed into the room, red-faced and scowling in his flannel pajamas. "Why are you two still awake?"

"I don't know," Brody said. "Why don't you tell us?"

"Why do little freshmen always have smart mouths?"

"I don't know," Brody said again. "Why are you such a dick?"

Anthony sat up and waited for a punch that never came. Instead of knocking Brody from his chair, Zach opened the door. "Lights off, little fresh meat," he said.

"Or I'm getting Mr. Hawley."

The next morning, Anthony woke up before the alarm could go off, avoided a couple of fresh tissues on the floor, and glared at his sleeping roommate. It was going to be a long year. Either Brody was an uncontrollable slob, or he was trying to push Anthony's buttons. He went to the bathroom, took a shower, brushed his teeth; came back to find Brody sill sleeping soundly. Good.

He dressed quietly. It was the first day of classes, the official beginning of his Belton career. Now was the time for khakis and loafers, time to find if MLK Junior High had taught him anything worth knowing. If he was sharp enough to hold his own with the rich and privileged, it might make his time at Belton a little easier. If he wasn't, then they would probably send him back home. And that would be fine with Anthony, too.

Brody farted and Anthony took one last quick look in the mirror, reluctantly shook his roommate awake, and then hurried out the door. The hallway was filling with dazed freshman boys, wrapped in towels and heading to the showers.

He went through the dormitory's double doors and sat on the front steps. It was cold, and frost had turned the grass white. If this was Maine in early September, then Anthony didn't want to be around in February. The doors opened behind him, and someone called him by the wrong name, telling him to go make up his bed.

"All right, man," Anthony said, but didn't move.

Zach sighed. "Come on, Tony, don't be a smart-ass little freshman. Do it now, so I can go to breakfast."

"Go on, I ain't stopping you. And quit calling me Tony, bitch. That's not my name."

Zach stared for a few seconds with his mouth hanging open. Then he turned around and stormed back into the dorm. He was probably telling Mr. Hawley, but Anthony didn't care. Until Zach learned how to show respect, the two of them were going to have problems.

Anthony took his time but finally went back inside, made his bed, and then headed to breakfast. He noticed Paul and Khalik walking ahead of him and quickly caught up. When they saw the black girl sitting alone outside the dining hall, the three of them walked even faster. Paul sat down next to her, and Anthony stood on the other side. She looked like a young Beyoncé and her hair smelled like citrus fruit.

"Excuse me?" she said, leaning away from Anthony but into Paul. "This ain't the A train. Give a sister some room."

Paul and Khalik grinned triumphantly and shouted, "Brooklyn!" at the same time.

Her name was Gloria, and she was a new tenth grader. A death in the family had delayed her arrival, and she had just gotten in the night before. Other than her roommate and a few other girls in her dorm, the three boys were the only people she'd talked to.

"Well, don't get your hopes up," Khalik said happily. "As far as black people go, you pretty much found all of us."

"Not everybody," she said, and smiled to herself. "George Fuller goes to school here, too, right?"

Khalik dribbled and then shot an invisible basketball. "You know Big G? Planet Brooklyn strikes again, ya heard?"

"Well, we ain't seen him yet," Paul said in a voice that was suddenly deep. "But that's why I came here, to help my man win a championship."

"Me, too," Khalik added, dribbling the ball again.

"What about you, baby?" Paul continued. "You got any game? 'Cause I can teach you."

Gloria stood and looked down at the top of his head. Paul stood, too, but still had to look up to her. "Don't worry, little fella," she said. "I got enough game for both of us."

Anthony suddenly felt shorter than usual, and he was tired of being on the outside looking in. "Wish they had them some football at this school," he offered. "Now that's my sport, right there."

Gloria looked back and forth between Paul and Khalik, and then settled her gaze on Anthony. "You wishin' they had dem some footbawl?" she said. "Where you from? Alabama?"

Anthony's face got warm, but he kept his voice even. "I'm from Cleveland," he said. "You know, Ohio?"

She rolled her eyes and said, "More like *Slow*-hio." Everyone laughed, including Anthony, who would have let the beautiful girl insult him every day of the week.

They went inside the dining hall and spotted George almost right away. He was huge and sitting at a table in the back of the room, along with another black boy and one that looked Puerto Rican. "Why does he have to be so damn fine?" Gloria said, and touched Anthony's shoulder.

"I don't know," he said, feeling suddenly jealous and reckless at the same time. "Let's go on over there and ask him." Anthony was pulling her along before she could answer. Paul and Khalik trailed behind them, whispering to each other. When they got close to the table, the older boys looked up. Anthony cleared his throat and introduced himself. "W'sup, man, I'm Ant Jones. You must be George, right?" He extended a palm, and the biggest boy slapped it.

"Nice to meet you," George said, but he was looking at Gloria. The other boys at his table were looking at her, too.

"This is Gloria," Ant continued, and then motioned to the other boys standing behind them. "This one right here is Paul. The other one is Khalik. They're all from Brooklyn, just like you, I guess."

Paul and Khalik quickly slapped George's hand, while Gloria shyly smiled. "How you doing?" she said, and then looked at the floor.

"I'm good, baby girl," George said, spreading his legs. "Especially right now." He grinned and she looked down again, trying to hide her happiness. "So you're from Brooklyn?" George continued. "What part?"

"Brownsville. What about you?"

"Bed-Stuy, do or die."

Paul hooted and so did Khalik. One of the boys sitting with George did it, too. Anthony frowned, but what else did he expect? "Everywhere I look, another New Yorker."

The Latino boy spoke up then and proudly thumped his chest. "No New York here," he said. "I come straight from the mean streets of Lawrence."

"Don't front, Hector," the other boy said, laughing. "They don't even have streets in that part of Massachusetts, mean or nice."

"Whatever, Jamaal," Hector said. "We got streets, and we got Latin Kings, too." He threw up signs with both of his hands, and Jamaal answered with stiff middle fingers.

Just then there came a commotion from near the front of the dining hall. Someone had dropped their dishes, and most of the kids were cheering. When he turned his attention back to the table, Anthony saw that George was looking at him. "So where you from, shorty rock?" George asked. "Boston?"

"Slow-hio," Khalik answered before Anthony could. "You can hear it in his country-ass voice."

Anthony glared. "I can beat that ass slow, too."

"Damn," George said while everyone else laughed. "Remind me not to piss you off. What part of Ohio you from? Cincinnati?"

"East Cleveland."

Jamaal's face lit up for a second, and he leaned across the table. "East Cleveland? I'm from East New York. You think they're the same?"

"I don't know," Anthony said, still wanting to punch Khalik. "Probably."

George looked back and forth between the two nodding boys and then started to nod himself. "Well, all right, Ant from East Cleveland," he said, standing up. "Believe it or not, around here you gotta look both ways before you cross the street, just like back at home." He bent down, put a hand on Gloria's shoulder, and squeezed. "You let me know if you need anything, baby girl. Day or night." Walking away, the big junior leaned into Jamaal. "Swear to God, son. She look just like Beyoncé."

Anthony's first class that day was Algebra I, and he left it feeling dizzy. The same thing was true for biology, history, and Spanish. The only exception was English, but even then most of the conversation went over his head. If it wasn't for the fact that Gloria was in there,

Anthony wouldn't have paid attention to anything.

And it was all of the talking that confused him the most. Kids had something to say about everything. It didn't matter if they had the right answer or not, or even if they kept to the topic; the teachers still let kids run their mouths until they ran out of words or until another student interrupted. Anthony had never experienced classes like that. Back at home, kids who asked too many questions usually got shut down or sent to the principal's office. And as for the ones who had all the answers, sometimes they got sent to the hospital.

So Anthony didn't ask any questions that day or for much of that first week of classes. He rarely raised his hand or made a comment. He felt invisible sometimes, but it didn't bother him at all. It was like his teachers knew it, too, and agreed to play along. He did finish all of his homework, though, and turned most of it in on time. Brody, on the other hand, was having trouble. If he wasn't somewhere getting high or kissing Venus, he was strumming his guitar and singing off-key. The only time he worked was during evening study hours, when teachers patrolled the dorms to make sure none of the kids were goofing off.

On one of those nights, Anthony and Brody sat at

their desks, reading an assignment for Mr. Hawley's English class. It was an old story about a black man in a segregated southern town, where he worked for a white family as a resident handyman. Although he was religious and often turned the other cheek, the man snapped one night and shot a lot of the people, black and white, young and old, he didn't care who he killed. When he ran out of bullets, the man stopped by a river and waited for the advancing mob. They shot him to pieces and then displayed the riddled body in a store window. Near the end of the story, back inside the dead man's modest room, it showed his Bible open to a passage about Judgment Day.

Anthony put down the book and looked at the words from a distance. They were as blurred as the man's final gesture. He could have escaped but took his boots off instead. It was like the man had wanted to get caught. Anthony glared at Brody, who, by the shocked look on his face, had also finished the reading.

"Bummer," Brody said, and flipped the book closed. Then he stared straight ahead and said nothing.

The next day, before English class, Anthony was apprehensive. Kids were abuzz over the reading and ready to talk about it. Mr. Hawley breezed in and dropped his briefcase on his desk, pulled the cap off a dry-erase marker, and wrote WHY? across the whiteboard.

Immediately a dozen hands flew up. And although they each expressed it in a dozen different ways, every kid agreed that racism had made the man kill.

"Interesting . . ." Mr. Hawley stopped behind Brody and put a hand on his shoulder. "Is that what you think, too?"

Brody shrugged. "Yeah, I guess."

Mr. Hawley glared. "You guess?"

"I mean, yes," Brody said, straightening up. "If you think about the time period, the place of African Americans on the social ladder, the way the white people mistreated and disrespected him in the story, it makes perfect sense that he would get fed up and go postal."

"Impressive," Hawley said, and moved on. Anthony agreed and stared at his roommate, who sat in a sudden patch of sunlight that came in through the window.

"Anyone disagree?" Hawley asked. No one raised a hand.

"What about the Bible?" Hawley continued, and

started moving again. This time he stopped directly behind Anthony. "Why did the author make the Bible so significant to the killer?"

The hands on his shoulders made Anthony jump. Hawley was looking down at him and benevolently smiling. "What about you, Mr. Jones? Anything to add?"

Everyone turned to look at him, and Anthony suddenly felt hot. "I don't go to church," he said, and stared at the table. Then he thought about something else from the story that had bothered him. It didn't have anything to do with the Bible, but it did poke holes in everyone's theory. Slowly, he raised his hand. "One thing," Anthony said. "If he was mad at white people for mistreating him, then why did he kill black people, too?"

Trouble came to the freshman floor on Friday, in the form of a sopping kid named Chris. Upperclassmen had pushed him around and thrown him into a brook, leaving him soaked and smelling awful. It was the latest run-in with the kids from Welch that had Anthony concerned. So far, he had managed not to get in any fights, but he was afraid that someone would test him.

Later, after Mr. Hawley had checked them all in for the night, Anthony and a few other ninth graders snuck out of their bunks and to Chris's room, to hear more about what had happened. "They called it Freshman Brook," Chris explained, not looking at anyone. "Told me not to fight, that it's sorta like school tradition to throw in the freshman boys . . . At least, that's what they told me."

One of the kids called it hazing, and a lot of them looked relieved. It was an acceptable and expected abuse, part of the prep-school world not mentioned in the catalogs. For Anthony and a few others, though, it didn't make any sense. He could never just let somebody punk him.

"I don't know about that one," Anthony said, more to himself than anyone else. "Somebody put their hands on me . . . I don't know."

"Right?" Paul added. "That's some craziness, son."

One boy suggested that they go talk to Zach, but Chris shook his head. "Zach was there when it happened," Chris said. "He didn't throw me in, but he didn't stop them, either."

At first it was silent but then Nate hissed, "We should go upstairs and put shaving cream on Zach's face!"

Brody laughed. "You guys gotta relax. . . . *Take a chill pill, on the ill will, while you still . . . feel . . .* Shit." He laughed again, and everyone looked at him.

"Nate's right, though," said a kid named Alex. "We should retaliate, but how? They're bigger than us, and they have us outnumbered. . . . We need a plan. . . ."

The boys looked at one another but didn't speak. Brody broke the silence with a drumroll. *"Outweighed and outnumbered . . . delaying our slumber . . . gotta figure a way, to make them all pay, for making Chris swim like a flounder . . ."* Someone belched. "Thanks," Brody continued. "I call that one 'Ode to a Flying Freshman Fish.'"

"No offense," Alex said, "but we've strayed off topic. Our mission is to devise a plan, not mock the bard."

"The what?"

"That's me," Brody said, bowing humbly. "Brody the bard, at your service. Bringing music to a deeply troubled world."

None of the talk made sense to Anthony. Just like in class, the way that he saw things seemed different from everyone else. No wonder he had never heard of hazing before. Back at home, it would get someone shot.

FIVE

"WAIT FOR ME," PAUL HOLLERED FROM BEHIND
him. "You act like they're gonna fire us."

"They might," Anthony said, not slowing down.
"Either that, or they're gon' put us with maintenance.
You feel like unclogging toilets on Saturdays?"

"Not me, son." Paul picked up the pace.

Anthony and Paul had work-study as part of their
financial-aid package. They washed dishes three morn-
ings a week to help cover the cost of tuition. After gob-
bling breakfast, they walked through the swinging
doors and into the kitchen, past the ovens, and into
the dish room.

"Turn that down," Paul groaned, already reaching

for an apron. "Don't wanna hear all that Spanish junk this early in the morning."

Unperturbed, Hector turned up the music. "This is Dominican music, Papi. Not Spanish."

"I don't care what it is. You making me feel like I'm in the Bronx."

There was laughter, and Hector returned to his station. Anthony wedged his way past George and grabbed an apron from a hook.

George looked down at Anthony and then at Paul. "Made you late again?"

Anthony nodded. "Dude be spending more time picking out clothes than my mother."

"Don't worry," George said, almost a little sadly. "He'll change."

"Change how?"

Just then one of the cooks came in and gave them all the sign. George raised the big sliding door above the counter until it locked into place, and sounds from the cafeteria rolled in. "Change how?" Anthony repeated.

"For the better," George said, and then winked at him. "Don't you know Belton makes everybody better?"

There was a steady stream of dirty dishes and then

the rush before morning assembly. The boys emptied bowls and scraped plates, stacked the dirty dining ware into special trays, and then ran them through the machine.

"Ever notice how there's only black people in here?" Hector said, leaning against the counter. "Serious, look around. How come don't no white boys work the kitchen?"

"'Cause we're on financial aid," Anthony said. "We need it and they don't."

"And you ain't even black, Ricky Martin," Paul said. "So chill."

They laughed and started pulling off their aprons. George stood in the doorway in front of them and cleared his throat. "They have white kids at Belton on financial aid, too," he said. "They just don't work in here, with us." He reminded them of the students in the bookstore and the library. Many of them didn't even have dark hair. "That's not the point, though," he continued. "Look at the percentages. For every one of them that's doing work-study, you have another three that can buy the whole damn school."

Anthony thought about his arrival on campus and all the expensive cars. He'd met kids who dined with diplomats and took family vacations in Greece. But so what? Sometimes he thought all their money made them soft, but that didn't make Anthony dislike them. George, on the other hand, was scowling. Anthony said, "Are you pissed just because some people here have money?"

"No," George snapped. "I'm pissed because we only got a spoonful of students of color, and every one of us is on financial aid. I'm pissed because it makes it look like every black person in the world is poor. And if they think we're all poor, then they probably think we're all stupid and eat watermelon, too."

"But we are poor, right?"

George glared at Paul and shook his head, rubbed a big hand down his face, and sighed. "That's not the point," he said evenly. "Let me put it another way. Where do you think financial aid comes from? And please don't say from washing dishes. . . ."

He waited, and the younger boys looked at one another. Then Paul said, "From nowhere. They just don't charge us."

George shook his head. "Every time these white kids pay their tuition, they pay a little bit of yours and mine, too. And don't think they don't know it, either."

Hector cried out, "That's fucked up, bro! I don't want them paying for me, I can pay it myself."

"No, you can't," Paul said. "So don't front. Just accept that cash and use it to your advantage." Hector thought for a second and nodded, then the two of them slapped hands.

Anthony wasn't swayed. "No such thing as a free lunch, though." He looked up at George. "So what do they want from us?"

"League championship," Paul interrupted, and shot an imaginary jumper. "Maybe two or three." Hector reached up and grabbed the invisible rebound while George glared joylessly at the two of them.

"You're a smart dude, Ant," George said, watching them play. "Twenty-five-twenty always expects something. Remember that."

Anthony nodded. "What's twenty-five-twenty?"

George grinned. "Think about the alphabet," he said. "Put the twenty-fifth letter with the twentieth. What you got?"

"Y and T," Anthony said, not seeing it at first. "Y. T. Why tea . . . ? Whitey?"

George smiled. "I knew you were smart. Twenty-five-twenty is a bitch up here, son. And like I said, they didn't bring you up here for free."

Anthony looked at the other two boys. Even without a ball, their game was competitive. "I don't play basketball. You know that."

"Don't matter, you will. What else you gonna do when winter comes, anyway? Join the ski team? Just remember what I said before, okay? Belton changes people."

"Yeah, for the better, right?" George didn't answer. Paul took another jump shot, and Hector swatted it away.

"Get that weak mess outta here!"

"Be real, son," Paul said. "Everybody know y'all Ricans can't jump."

Anthony laughed with them to hide his worry. He would have to play basketball, George was right about that. Belton freshmen were required to play at least two team sports, and since Anthony was already skipping the fall, he had to either ski or shoot hoops in the winter. The problem was that he was terrible. When the season started, he would be the only kid of color without a varsity uniform.

He looked at George. "Can you teach me?"

"Swear to God, Ant," George said, smiling in

disbelief. "You need to clean out your ears. What you think I'm doing right now?"

Later that day in health class, the teacher showed a documentary about cigarettes, narrated by a woman who talked through a hole in her throat. Anthony watched from a seat on the floor, next to a girl who smoked and always smelled like it.

"You know what that looks like, right?" a boy whispered from behind them. "A butthole. You know, like a hole for her butts?"

"She doesn't smoke through it, jerk," the girl said, and then shifted uncomfortably. "Starting today, I'm quitting. . . . Today or however long it takes to finish my carton."

The period ended and Anthony went on to the next class, thinking of the movie, the girl who'd sat next to him, and mixed messages. The handbook stated that Belton was a smoke-free school. But dorm parents handed out flashlights to smokers at night and directed them to off-campus spots near the roadway, where they could stand in the darkness and puff. The same was true for how the school handled hazing and sex. In a way, the whole place was a farce. On weekdays it was a lot like the catalog: smiling kids and happy faculty interacting in classrooms; crowds cheering the teams on the fields. But weekends at Belton were a lot like full moons, and most of the students were werewolves.

That night, Anthony sat at dinner with Brody and Nate, half listening to them insult each other, feeling a bit more settled in at the school but still nowhere close to contented. He missed home but didn't always think about it, which usually brought on rounds of guilty phone calls. He had already burned through two months of laundry quarters in just a little over four weeks.

George walked into the dining hall then, slapped hands with some of the kitchen staff, and stopped briefly to talk with the headmaster. Then he went and sat alone at a table but didn't keep his solitude for long. A steady trickle of kids, from athletes to burnouts, came to sit with him or offer high fives.

"Earth to Tony?" It was Brody, and he was waving his chicken.

"Huh?"

"Never mind. What about you, Nate? Wanna go to North Conway tomorrow? My dad said I could bring a friend."

"I dunno," Nate said haltingly, "your dad seems kinda weird. . . ."

"Forget it."

". . . He kinda has that look."

"I said forget it. Jesus Christ, dude, you just go on and on. Maybe you're the weird one. Ever think about that?"

Anthony turned to watch King George, surrounded by his court of twenty-five-twenty, calmly eating his food. A blond girl rushed over with a slice of apple pie, put it down, and sat on his lap. For all of his warnings about the nature of white people, George seemed to have a lot of them as friends.

". . . Tony?" It was Brody again, and it was clear that he was getting annoyed.

"I told you to stop calling me that."

"Sorry, *Anthony*. So you'll go, right?"

He thought about the day he met Brody's parents, the way they'd made a joke of his last name, how Mr. Lavallee had seemed to take pleasure in almost breaking his hand. Anthony didn't want to see them again any more than he suspected they wanted to see him. "Naw, man," he said, deliberately not looking at his roommate. "You can count me out."

Across the room, George got up and left, the blond girl draped over him. They walked past the headmaster's table, where a few of the men sitting there either looked away from the couple or grinned.

Nate made an obscene gesture. "Where do you think they're going?"

"Anywhere they want," Anthony said in quiet awe.

The dining hall slowly emptied. Kids left in pairs and in threes and in groups, some determined to screw or kill brain cells. And the teachers, jacked up from cups of dinner coffee, went out to try and stop them from succeeding.

Anthony soon found himself at the pay phone on his floor, waiting for the operator. On the wall, someone had drawn a smiling penis with running legs, not far from Nate's name, scrawled in the same color. Someone else had drawn a pair of cartoon bears, dancing in a field of mushrooms. And there was something in a language that Anthony didn't recognize, next to a phone number with too many digits.

"Go ahead, sir," the operator said, coming back. "And thank you for using AT&T."

The phone clicked, and then Anthony's mother said, "Hello?"

"Hey, Ma. What's up?"

"I've been wondering the same thing," she said

happily. "You forget our number?"

"I know. Sorry. They keep us pretty busy, and like I told you last time, this is the only phone on the floor."

"Well, we gon' have to see about getting you a cell phone, 'cause we need to stay in touch."

He agreed but didn't say anything about reception in the valley. "So what's going on with you?" he asked. "How's life in Cleve-burg?"

"I'm pretty fair, baby, just going to work every day, like always. You know don't nothing change around here but the weather. What I wanna know about is those grades."

He closed his eyes and thought about all the Cs he'd earned so far, except for algebra, which had dipped down into the D range. He still had time to turn things around before report cards went out, but he would have to work like his life depended on it. "Everything's fine, Ma," he said. "No failures and no fights."

"And your roommate, what's his name, Brodney? How are you two getting along?"

"Better," Anthony said, and then thought about it. The morning Kleenex had finally disappeared, and since Brody's grades had been pretty bad, too, he was spending more time in the library. "Yeah, I guess it's been a lot better between us," he continued. "I still spend most of my time with the other black kids, though."

He couldn't see it, but Anthony could hear the frown in her voice. "You got black friends back here," his mother snapped. "Don't be wasting time up there with people who cain't do nuthin' for you. How many times I gotta tell you that?"

"Okay."

"For all you know, that Brodney boy could be the key to you getting a job or going to college . . ."

"You're right, Ma. Okay."

". . . Shoot, wish I had me that kinda chance. You best believe I wouldn't blow it."

Anthony picked up a discarded marker from the floor. "I won't blow it, Ma," he said. "I promise." He tested the felt on his fingertip, and it left a black dot. "Anybody else home?" He scribbled aimlessly on the wall.

"Darnell was here a few minutes ago," she said. "You just missed him."

"Oh . . ." He stopped his circles and put the marker down. One of the dancing bears had been disfigured.

"What's wrong, baby?"

"Huh? Nothing."

"You sure?"

"Yeah. I'm fine, Ma." There was a twang in her voice. Not quite southern fried but still country, just the same. He supposed it had been there all the time, only he hadn't noticed it before.

"Don't worry, baby," she said. "Thanksgiving's coming. When was the last time you had some yams and some cornbread? Some black-eyed peas and collard greens?"

"I really couldn't tell you, Ma. They don't even have grits up here."

She laughed and said, "Poor baby. You must be 'bout as skinny as a stick. Well, we gon' have to really do it up for you next month."

"That long? I wanna come home right now." He listened to the doors around him opening and closing, watched the passing kids who'd come in for the night. "I miss everybody."

"We miss you, too, but don't go getting all soft. Stay strong and do what you gotta do."

"I will."

He hung up just as Brody stomped past him, soaking wet. "What happened to you?"

Brody didn't answer but kept walking. Anthony followed him to their room and closed the door. "Seriously, man. What happened?"

"Guess?" Brody emptied his backpack, dumped the soggy papers into the garbage can, and put his open books facedown on the radiator. He peeled off his clothes and threw them into the corner. Stink rose from the pile like swamp gas. "I fucking hate this place, dude." He put on dry clothes and sat at his desk, staring straight ahead.

"How'd they get you?"

"On my way from the library. I walked into it like an idiot."

"Was that big kid with the ponytail there? Seth McCarthy?"

"Oh, yeah," Brody said hatefully. "Zach, too. They carried us past Mr. Voght and the old bastard made a joke about it." He went to the mirror and parted his hair. "Hit my head on a rock or something."

Anthony looked at him. "You just said us. Did they get somebody else, too?"

Brody nodded and sat down again. "Khalik. And he was screaming like a baby."

Anthony took off. Seconds later he was down the

hall and in front of Mr. Hawley's apartment, pressing the buzzer. The door opened and the man stuck out his head. "Can I help you?"

"We gotta talk," Anthony said. "Right now."

Mr. Hawley stepped aside, and Anthony stormed past him, slapped the kitchen table hard, and paced the room. "Somebody better do something."

Looking stunned, Mr. Hawley shut the door and leaned against it. "What's going on?"

"Freshman Brook. That's what's going on. You better stop these people before I do." He told Hawley what had happened, making sure to mention his roommate's head and the fact that a few kids had been thrown in twice.

"Twice?" Hawley seemed more surprised than upset. A smile pulled at the corners of his mouth.

"You think it's funny, huh?" Anthony said. "It figures."

"Not funny, Tony, but come on. Nobody got hurt, right?"

"What about Brody's head? That's not hurt enough for you?"

Hawley pressed his lips together. "Okay, you're right. But come on, Tony. You know what I mean."

"No, I don't. And stop calling me Tony. That's not my damn name!"

Mr. Hawley's mouth snapped shut, and all the fun left his face. "I'm sorry," he said. "I'm sorry, Anthony, okay? But if you ever speak to me that way again, I'll have to take disciplinary action."

"Why? 'Cause it's in the handbook, right? Just like this is supposed to be a smoke-free campus, but then you tell people where they can have cigarettes. Why don't you take some 'disciplinary action' with those fools doing the hazing, instead of threatening me?"

"I'm not threatening you."

"And you ain't threatening McCarthy, either," Anthony said. "That's okay, let one of them put his hands on me."

Hawley sighed and pinched his temples. "You can't fight here, Anthony. We take that very seriously."

"No, you don't, 'cause if you did there wouldn't be people getting thrown in brooks and getting their heads dunked in toilets."

Hawley smiled again, but it faded quickly. "That's not fighting, Anthony, that's hazing. You know, just older kids giving the young ones a little grief. . . . Look, I know it sucks, but Freshman Brook is a tradition.

Hell, I got thrown in when I went to school here. I was pissed for a while, too. But the next three years, I more than made up for what happened to me. You'll get your turn."

"So you're not gonna do anything? And that fat punk of a proctor, you're not gonna do anything about him, either?"

"I wouldn't put it like that. Jesus, Anthony, relax!" He tried to put a hand on Anthony's shoulder, but the boy shrugged it off.

"Don't they have something about hazing in the handbook? Didn't you make us fill out a form?"

Hawley stared back at him but didn't say anything.

"Just what I thought. Tell you what, Mr. Hawley, and God is my witness: If any of those dudes puts their hands on me, whatever happens is your fault, not mine."

Hawley bunched his hair in both hands and groaned. Anthony waited, but the man didn't say anything. From the hallway outside came the sound of Zach barking orders.

"Fine," Anthony said, walking to the door. "Just don't be surprised if you have to get another proctor, then. The one you got now might not make it."

SIX

ANTHONY WOKE UP THE NEXT MORNING AND TOOK
a shower, working the plan in his mind while he
washed behind his ears. His mother had been proud
the day he'd washed his ears without her asking, and
she clapped the first time he rode a bike without train-
ing wheels. He wondered what she'd do if she knew
what he was setting up. Would she be happy or tell
him to pack his bags?

In the room, he looked at himself in the mirror.
There was fuzz coming in above his lip, but it was hard
to see against his skin. Kids at home used to tease him
about his complexion, said they couldn't find him in

the dark unless he was smiling. He had expected to hear the same jokes at Belton, but so far no one had seemed to care.

Someone knocked on the door and told Anthony that he had a call. He got dressed and went to the pay phone cubby. "Hello?"

"Hello to you too, nigga. W'sup?"

"Floyd?" Anthony sat down and grinned. "About time you called me for a change," he said. "I was fi'n to write you off."

Floyd laughed. "It ain't like that. Every time I try to call, the line be busy. . . . So what's poppin', playa? What's the word?"

"Same as the last time I talked to you, man. Nothing. Go to breakfast, go to class, go to study hall, go to sleep."

"Damn, nigga. Sound like you in the joint."

"Might as well be." Anthony told him about visual check-ins with the weekend duty crew, the work-study jobs and room inspections. "Plus, we got night security that be walking around campus . . . couldn't get away with nothing if I tried."

"What I tell you, man?" Floyd said smugly. "That's

exactly why I ain't up there with you."

Anthony looked at the artwork on the walls around him. Someone had scribbled out the running penis and written UNCOOL! underneath it. "We got girls here," he continued. "That's a plus."

"Yeah, man, all them snowflakes. I need me a fat booty, not a flat one."

"Same here," Anthony said. "We got this girl from New York who look like Beyoncé. I'm trying to holler at her."

"That's what's up, playa. Get yours. Had a couple fiends over at Shane's crib yesterday. Told them hoes to kiss each other and they did! Just like some shit off the internet."

Anthony laughed. "Be careful, man. You too young to be somebody's daddy."

"Don't worry about me, playa. I come wrapped or I don't come at all. The last thing I want is some baby or the HIV." Floyd paused, and when he spoke again his voice had lost its sparkle. "Seem like everybody and they momma got the bug, man, even these two girls in my homeroom. . . . Niggas 'round here always be dropping like flies, from one thing or another."

Anthony thought about home and all the things that

could go wrong there, thought about Mookie and all the gunshots at night. Just like a lot of other things in East Cleveland, even sex was killing its teenagers. "That's some scary shit," he said absently. "I cain't even imagine."

Floyd laughed, but Anthony could tell by the tone that his best friend wasn't amused. "You cain't imagine?" Floyd said. "Nigga, you grew up here. Being scared of E.C. is like being scared of yourself."

He looked at the scribble on the wall again and fought an urge to make it darker. "I'm not scared," Anthony said. "I just said it was scary. There's a difference."

Floyd let out a long sigh. "Whatever, man . . . anyway, you seen your boy yet? That writer?"

Anthony hesitated. His mind was in a hundred different places. Then the name came to him all at once. "Stephen King? Naw, he don't live nowhere near here."

"Oh . . . what about them stories, you wrote any new ones?"

"Naw," Anthony answered guiltily. "I ain't really had the time yet. . . ."

"Ain't had the time?" Floyd laughed his hollow laugh again and then said he had to go. Before he hung up, he asked Anthony a last question. "If the place is like jail and you hate it so much, why in the world is you still up there?"

He was running into the gym when Gloria stormed out of it, her face a mix of frustration and anger. When Anthony asked her what was wrong, she shouted "GUESS!" and kept walking. Anthony knew that she was talking about George, and the news couldn't have made him any happier. Brooklyn had bound them on the day they had met, but now Gloria and George were oil and water. She thought he was a politician and a low-key Uncle Tom, while George called her a nosy troublemaker.

George was already on the court, shooting three-pointers from the top of the key that barely moved the net. When that rack was empty, he moved on to the next one and tossed in perfect turnaround jumpers from the baseline.

"Thought you weren't gonna make it," George said without breaking his rhythm. "If you want to get better, you have to practice every day. No excuses."

Anthony joined him on the court and racked the loose balls. Then he grabbed one of them and quickly dribbled two laps, staying low and keeping his head up, alternating hands after every few bounces, just like George had showed him. "I saw Gloria on my way in here," he said. "She looked mad."

George sniffed and flipped in the last shot underhanded. "That girl has serious problems," he said. "She's mad at the whole world."

"Maybe so, but I think she's especially mad at you." He finished his laps and went to the foul line, shot free throws while George snagged the rebounds.

"You're getting better," George said after Anthony made a couple. "Just find a routine that works and stick with it. That's the key to everything."

"Everything, huh?" Anthony said, and concentrated. His next three shot attempts missed badly. "Guess I ain't found the right routine yet."

He moved on to right-handed layups and then left ones, after that it was midrange jumpers over George's outstretched arm. By the time he finished defensive slides and rebounding drills, Anthony was soaked in sweat. George kept after him, though, and made him play through the discomfort. An hour later, when Anthony had completed his mini practice, the two boys sat on the bench and drank from water bottles, looking up at the league championship banners from the late 1990s.

"We can do it this year," George announced, and smacked a fist into his palm. "All we need to do is play good defense and get the ball to me."

Anthony nodded. He didn't know what the competition was like, but he had faith in George. It seemed everything that George touched turned to gold. Everything except for Gloria. "Let me ask you a question," Anthony said. "What's the story between you and your homegirl?"

George shrugged and took a long drink. "There is no story," he said, and took a sip. "She's jealous. That's all."

"Jealous? Jealous of what?"

"Of me," George said matter-of-factly. "She don't understand how a black dude from Brooklyn can come up here and have so much juice."

Anthony nodded. He didn't understand it either, but he was trying to learn by watching George both on and off the basketball court. "I think there's more to it than that," he said. "I think she likes you. No, scratch that. I think she *used* to like you. She used to like you, and now she cain't stand your ass." He laughed and unscrewed the top from his bottle. When he drank, the smell of plastic was strong.

George shrugged and took off his sneakers, set them to the side, and then put on boots. "I know how she feels about me," he said. "Or used to feel." He shrugged again and put on his sweatshirt, crossed his arms over his chest, and shook his head. "Don't get me wrong, the girl is fine. I mean, movie-star fine and everything. But she just has too much *attitude* for me, know what I'm saying? I can't be dealing with all that attitude while I'm trying to get a college scholarship. Shit, I have a plan."

"Attitude, huh?" Anthony thought about it and nodded. Gloria could come off a little rough, just like Shameeka back at home. But she was smarter than Shameeka and looked a hundred times better. "There ain't enough attitude in the world to make me say no to that," he said absently. "Whatever she dish out, I would just take it and smile."

"Then you should go for it," George said, standing up. "Maybe you can rub off on her some, help her fit in and not be such a bitch all the time."

"Maybe." Anthony thought about the hazing and

his grades so far in classes, the way he alternated between liking his roommate and wanting to throw him through a wall. He wasn't fitting in any better than Gloria. It would be a case of the blind leading the blind. "Let me ask you another question," he said as they left the gym. "What's the deal with Freshman Brook?"

George looked down at him and shrugged. "Tradition, son. That's what it is. I guess they been doing it for the last hundred years."

"So I heard."

George laughed. "Don't worry about it. It's only water."

"You mean rotten water," Anthony said. "You shoulda smelled my roommate's clothes." Then he thought about Khalik and how powerless he must have felt. They had stripped him of his stories and all his Brooklyn bluster, tossed him in the brook, and taken away his clout. Anthony looked at George, who wasn't laughing anymore but still grinning, walking easily in long strides. "I don't get you, man," Anthony said. "One minute you warning me against white people and now you act like I should let 'em do whatever they want."

"Not whatever they want," George said. "But you

need to be careful, choose your battles. This is one you can't win."

Anthony hawked and spat as far as he could. It landed in a shiny blotch on the path ahead of them. "So you don't think I can win, huh?"

"You might. But winning one little thing might make you lose it all."

That night Anthony lay awake in bed, eyes fixed on the ceiling but looking past it. He was bothered by George's warning: win the battle, lose the war. Anthony wasn't going to let anyone throw him in a brook. And he would never let them dunk his head in a toilet or make him take a cold shower fully clothed. What did any of that have to do with getting into college? How would letting them abuse him win Anthony anything except more contempt and cruelty? George was smart, but his advice was stupid. Anthony had a plan, and he was sticking to it.

He was sound asleep when Zach burst into the room, banging on things and yelling. "Get up, freshman fish! Emergency meeting in the hallway, right now!"

Brody got up and left the room on groggy legs, but Anthony stayed where he was. "What emergency?"

"You'll see," Zach answered. "Now let's go."

"Why? So you and your friends can try something? Naw, man. Go on, somewhere."

Zach sighed. "Are you coming or not?"

"Not."

"Your funeral." Zach stormed into the hallway, leaving the door wide open behind him. Seconds later, Mr. Hawley walked in. He looked angry and disappointed.

"What's the matter with you?" he snapped. "Too good to join everyone else?"

Anthony shrugged and jumped down from his bunk. "I thought it was a trick."

"A trick?" Hawley shook his head. "Yeah, it's a trick. Now let's go."

Anthony followed him into the hallway and saw the other freshmen. Some were in pajamas and others in their underwear; some seemed wide-awake while others slept on their feet.

"What time is it?" Hawley demanded while he paced up and down the lines. Someone said that it was 1:47, and the scowling dorm parent nodded. "That's right," he said, "almost two in the morning." He motioned to Zach, who was standing next to a big pile of cleaning supplies. "Two o'clock in the morning and I'm out here playing babysitter with a bunch of would-be Rembrandts and comedians. . . . Do you guys write on your walls back at home? Do your parents like to see cartoon genitalia?"

Someone giggled, and Hawley pulled him from the line. "Grab a bucket, Mr. Miller, since you think this is so funny." The boy jumped to the pile, and Hawley looked at everyone else. "I want it clean. The bathroom, the pay phone, your desks; everywhere someone was dumb enough to write something smart, I want it spotless."

The kids grabbed supplies and started cleaning. Anthony and Paul worked together, in the phone nook. "Mr. H is wilding, son," Paul said, barely touching the wall with his sponge. "We should report him for slave labor."

Anthony grinned and sprayed foam onto the dancing bear. It bubbled and ran down the wall in muddy lines. "At least it's coming off," he said, wiped, and sprayed again. "I thought some of this stuff was permanent."

Paul stopped moving his arm, cocked his head to one side, and looked at Anthony. "You're a funny dude," he said. "You know that?"

"Funny how?"

"One minute you walk around here like you're mad at the world and the next you clean graffiti at two in the morning with a smile on your face. I don't get you, man."

Anthony sprayed again and thought about it, not sure if he should take Paul's words as an insult or a compliment. "I'm used to this," he said finally. "Back at home, my mother be waking us up to clean all the time."

Paul shook his head and rubbed his sponge on the wall again. "Your moms sound serious, kid. Remind me not to stay at your house."

Anthony laughed and moved to another drawing. Maxine Jones *was* serious, but only because she cared. Suddenly he missed her and everyone else at home. He thought of calling, but it would only make him miss them more.

Paul had left the nook but was still only a few feet away, sitting on the floor and pretending to rub the baseboard. Anthony brought his can and rag over and sat next to him. "You going home for Thanksgiving?"

"Yeah," Paul said, and smiled dreamily. "I'm gonna eat myself to death."

"Me, too," Anthony said. "I might mess around and not even come back, you know? Just stay there and eat . . ." He found a mark on the wall next to him, sprayed it, and wiped the spot clean. He thought about asking Paul if he ever got homesick, if he found the unwritten rules at Belton just as confusing as the handbook. He didn't, though. Another kid came over with a sponge.

He got back to the room and immediately noticed the difference. Brody had separated the beds and put his on the other side of the little space. It was no longer right under Anthony's but at the same time seemed much closer. "You like?" Brody asked from his new spot. "I was wiping things down when the thought came to me: With my bed over here, we can see each other when we talk."

"Yeah," Anthony said, and climbed under his covers. The bed was still high but not high enough. "Next time, just tell me before you make a change."

"No problem," Brody said. "We can move it back, if you want to. I just thought it might be cool."

"It is, don't worry about it. You just surprised me, that's all." Anthony wanted to be mad, but he couldn't. In his heart he knew that his roommate meant well.

"You excited about Thanksgiving?"

"Not really, dude," Brody said, sitting up. "A lot of bad food and worse family, stuffed together in a room and trying to get along." He flipped the hair from his eyes. "At least I'll get to hang with my friends."

"Friends," Anthony said, thinking of Floyd and everyone at home. "What would we be without 'em?"

"I dunno," Brody said. "Falling trees in a forest with nobody to catch us, nobody to watch us or even hear us scream on the way down . . ."

Anthony looked at him. "Man, what in the hell are you smoking?"

"Dude!" Brody said, and then started laughing. "I dunno, but it's good!"

The next morning, Anthony ate brunch with Paul and Khalik. They knew about his crush on Gloria and offered their Brooklyn advice.

"Just step to her," Paul said. "Be like, 'Yo, baby girl, you know I like you. What's up?'"

"He tried to," Khalik blurted. "But she couldn't see him, standing down there by her kneecaps."

They slapped hands and Anthony cut pieces from his waffle, watching the front door.

Khalik said "Seriously, son. You know she's too tall for you, right? Why don't you go after somebody different?"

"Why don't you?"

"Because he can't," Paul said. "That's why he's messing with you. Go for yours, Anthony Ant. Every man should climb his own mountain . . . even if he need special shoes."

Anthony stuck a fork into his eggs. He didn't care about the short jokes or if they thought he didn't have a chance with Gloria. The person he'd been waiting for had just come into the room, surrounded by all of his bullying friends.

"So I heard you had some static the other night," Anthony said, looking at Khalik. Then he pinched his nose and acted like he was drowning. "How did it feel under all that stinky water? Come on, killa, did any get in your mouth?" Khalik didn't say anything. Anthony tilted his chin toward McCarthy's table. "It was them, right? They the ones that violated you?"

"Shut up."

"I'm surprised you let them do it to you," Anthony continued. "How you let them treat you like a punk and get away with it? What happened to all those bad-ass stories about Brooklyn?"

Khalik balled his fists and stood up. "Kiss my ass, Slow-hio."

Anthony jumped to follow him. From behind, he could hear Paul pushing away from the table, too.

McCarthy saw them coming and said something to his friends. They all looked at the approaching boys and laughed.

"How you doing, Seth?" Anthony said. "How's your food?"

McCarthy looked down at his plate and then at Anthony. "It's fine. Why? Did you do something to it?"

"Not me . . . but somebody could have. You never know around here."

McCarthy smiled and took a big bite from his omelet. "It's good. Work-study kids don't cook, Tony. But nice try."

"My name's Ant. I don't know no Tony."

"You don't know *any* Tony," McCarthy corrected. "You're a Belton man now, time to speak proper English." He raised a haughty eyebrow while his friends laughed. "Anything else, or does that conclude our lesson for the day?"

"I want to see the brook," Anthony said flatly. "People

say you know how to get there."

McCarthy looked at Khalik. "Ask your buddy. We showed him the way the other night."

"So I heard," Anthony said, "and now I want you to show me."

McCarthy frowned. "You *want* me to take you down there?"

"Bring your little friends, too," Anthony said. "The more the merrier."

McCarthy checked out Paul and Khalik. "What about your friends? Do they want to see it, too?"

The Brooklyn kids nodded. "Like I already told you," Anthony said. "The more the merrier."

McCarthy faced his crew, and they all leaned close together. Then he turned around and said, "See you on the soccer field in half an hour."

"That's what's up."

Anthony and his friends went back to Kaster and beat on freshman doors. They couldn't find Brody but got five other kids. They found McCarthy on the soccer field, close to the woods, along with six older boys, including Zach. Anthony stopped in front of them. "We're here."

"So I see," McCarthy answered. "Let's go." He walked

into the forest, and the two groups followed; juniors and seniors on the right side of the trail, Anthony and the other freshmen on the left. Kids from each camp threatened violence to the other, but they shouted out of grinning mouths.

"So what's the plan?" Paul asked, walking next to Anthony. "Half these fools think this is a joke."

"I know. It's crazy."

"What if they don't have your back?"

"You still got it, right?"

"Yeah, son," Paul said. "I don't swim too good, though."

Anthony told him not to worry. "If this works out the way I want it to, you won't ever get near the water."

The trees thinned and the path took them into an open area, covered in bushes and tall grass. "Over here." McCarthy led them over a little hill to a rickety bridge. Rancid water rolled slowly beneath it, foaming white against the bank.

"That's not a brook," one freshman said. "That's a toxic waste spill."

Khalik agreed. "Word life, son," he said to the older boys. "Somebody gonna buy me new sneakers."

Someone shouted, "Bullshit!" and the groups quickly

divided. Anthony and Paul stood in front of the freshmen, while McCarthy and Zach led the others.

Zach said, "Ready for a swimming lesson?"

"Not from you, you fake-ass proctor."

"Eat shit, little freshman!"

"Make me," Anthony said, and raised his fists. "I'm right here."

Everyone shouted after that, spraying spit and insults. But just like the banter on their walk to the water, it was just talk. "So that's it?" Anthony said during a lull. "All these threats and I'm still dry as I wanna be."

"You mean as dry as I want you to be," McCarthy said. "All I have to do is give the word."

"Well, give it, then. I'm tired of all this talking." He waited, but McCarthy didn't speak or move.

Paul laughed. "This dude is weak, yo. A little girl with a mustache."

"For real," Anthony said. "He probably gotta squat to take a piss."

McCarthy lunged and grabbed Anthony by the arm. "Got you, you little shit!"

Got you, too, Anthony thought, and then punched him in the eye.

McCarthy yelped and covered his face, pulled his

hands away, and stared down at the palms. The rest of the boys looked on in stunned silence.

"You hit me," McCarthy said.

"You tried to throw me in the brook!"

McCarthy pressed a hand to his eye again and winced. "Why did you do that? What the hell's wrong with you?"

Anthony wanted to finish his plan: throw McCarthy or one of his friends into the brook. But something stopped him from doing anything else, and it was more than McCarthy's odd reaction. Even the freshmen were looking at Anthony differently, like he had just kicked a puppy off a rooftop.

All the boys cleared out except for Paul and Khalik, who stood next to Anthony, looking stunned.

"You see that shit?" Khalik asked, shaking his head in disbelief.

"I saw it," Paul said. "But I don't know what I saw."

Anthony looked at them and then the empty path. What had just happened? Why hadn't his classmates carried him off on their shoulders? "He grabbed me first, right?" Anthony asked, just to be sure that his memory was straight. When his friends nodded, he nodded, too. "Good. 'Cause I was just defending myself."

They started back, and even though Khalik proclaimed him victorious, Anthony could only think of George's warning. Yes, he had won, but what had he lost in the process?

News of the confrontation traveled quickly. By evening, Anthony found judgment everywhere he went. He had an anger problem. He couldn't take a joke. Some kids weren't sure if they were safe around him. They wanted the school to do something.

That evening, Mr. Hawley pulled Anthony from the common room and brought him down to his apartment. Once inside, he grimly closed the door. "I wish you would have listened to me," Hawley said. "We take fighting very seriously here."

Anthony protested. "I was just defending myself, Mr. Hawley. I told him not to touch me, and he went and did it anyway. Ask Paul and Khalik. A whole bunch of people saw it."

Hawley was nodding before Anthony finished. "I know. I already checked around . . . talked to the dean of students, too." He told Anthony to take a seat. "You drink coffee?"

"Coffee's cool."

Mr. Hawley brought two steaming mugs to the table

and sat one of them in front of Anthony. Then he went back for a carton of half and half, a bowl of sugar, and a spoon. "Here you go," Mr. Hawley said and sat down.

Anthony took a sip and then put the spoon to work. With the right amount of sugar and enough cream to cool it, he could make a cup of coffee taste like candy.

"Jeez," Hawley said. "You're gonna be bouncing off the walls."

"I'll be all right. This is good; still not sweet enough, though." Anthony dumped in a couple more spoonfuls, stirred, sipped, and sighed. "That's better."

Hawley laughed, and Anthony laughed along with him. But then he remembered the circumstances. "So," Anthony said, unsure if he wanted to hear what was next. "How much trouble am I in?"

Mr. Hawley put his cup down. "You're both on behavioral probation for the rest of the marking period. You're not to talk to each other or interact in any way, unless it's to express an apology. . . ." He picked up his mug and sipped. "Like that's gonna happen."

Anthony waited for more, but that was the end of it: a slap on the wrist for a punch in the face. "What about him, though? I won't just stand there if he comes at me."

"You don't need to worry about Seth McCarthy," Mr. Hawley said, laughing. "I don't think that kid has ever been more afraid in his life."

Anthony suppressed a smile. "What about Zach? I don't know how you expect me to listen to him anymore."

"You're right," Hawley said, and ran a hand through his hair. "Guess I'm going to have a talk with him, too." He opened the door, and Anthony stepped out into the hall. Before he walked away, Hawley called him back.

"Hey. How would you feel about being my proctor next year?" Hawley asked. "I could show you how to apply for it, if you want."

"Why? So I can be like Zach?"

"No," Hawley said. "So you can be the opposite of him. Zach got teased a lot last year, and I guess the power is getting to him. It happens to people sometimes. Even good ones." He put a hand on Anthony's shoulder. "Not you, though. I can tell. You have a strong sense of justice." Hawley grinned. "So what do you say?"

"Maybe," Anthony answered. "Let me think about it."

SEVEN

"I DON'T GET IT, MAN," ANTHONY SAID SINCERELY,
and not for the first time that afternoon. A couple of
weeks had passed since his run-in with McCarthy, and
some people still treated him like a terrorist. Even fel-
low freshmen gave him a wide berth or apologized
if they accidentally touched him. If it hadn't been for
Brody and a couple of others, Anthony wouldn't have
had any friends at all. "Seriously, man," he said again.
"I don't get it."

George looked up from his Spanish book and sighed.
He had let Anthony hang out in his room a lot since
the incident, but it was clear that George was getting
tired of the company. "What don't you get this time?"

"Everything," Anthony said. "I mean, why is everybody tripping so hard, like I carry an ax or something?"

"Because in their eyes, you do. How many times do I have to tell you, son? Twenty-five-twenty is a bitch."

Anthony looked around the living space. George had his own bathroom and an oversized bed, hidden microwave in the closet, unseen television and fridge. Everyone knew that he had the contraband, even his proctor and dorm parent. But Mr. Rockwell was also his basketball coach, which allowed George a lot of latitude. "I'm talking about the other freshmen," Anthony continued. "Not a single one of them has been in the brook since it happened, and do they thank me for it? No. They treat me like I'm some kind of psycho. . . . Forget these people, man. My friends back at home wouldn't do me like that."

"But you're not at home anymore," George said. "You're in Maine, son. Belton Academy, established in 1844. I told you what would happen, but did you listen?" He closed his book, stood up, and grabbed the empty laundry basket from the floor. "Last load. Hold it down."

Anthony stretched out on the bed and thought about

the last month and a half. Plane rides and canoe trips; midnight study sessions with ramen noodles and gallons of Coke. He had come to know some of the Belton kids as well as his friends at home, from how their shit smelled in the morning to what kept them awake at night. But now there was a strain on everything because he had crossed an invisible line.

George returned and shooed Anthony off the bed, dumping the basket of clothes in his place. He started folding. "Gotta do it now, before they get wrinkled."

Anthony looked around the room that was more like an apartment, at the books and the trophies and all the photographs of George, smiling with friends of all colors. "I need to know how you do it," he said.

"Do what? Fold shirts?"

"Naw, man . . . tell me how you got everybody on your side."

George left his clothes and straddled a chair backward, resting his arms across the top. "Let me get this straight, you want me to show you how to get along with white people?"

"And still be myself, yeah."

George winked. "You can't. I told you that already. Around here, you have to be somebody else. More than one person, really." He held up one of his hands. "Five things," he said, and lowered a digit as he counted each one. "First and foremost, don't ever hit anybody, no matter how much they piss you off. I don't need to tell you why because you already know. Second, smile instead of scowling all the time, like you're mad at the world. The minute these people start feeling unsafe, brothers start getting sent home."

"Has that happened before?"

"More than you think. To tell the truth, I'm surprised you're still around."

"Me, too," Anthony said. "Somebody must be looking after me."

"That's good. Without Coach Rockwell watching my back, I would have been gone a long time ago." He stopped and looked somewhere far off. Then he blinked a couple of times.

"Third," George continued, "hit those books, son, and hit 'em hard. There's nothing more powerful in this world than a black man who uses his brain. And fourth, get to know these people. Learn their hobbies, where they come from, and what their parents do for a living. You never know when it all might come in handy." George stopped talking and arched his eyebrows, leaving his rigid middle finger still standing all alone.

"What's the last one? You said five things, right?"

George waved the finger back and forth. "You're right," he said. "This last one is the most important: No matter how much time you spend with them and how hard they try to do it, most of the kids here will never really know you." He put the finger down.

Anthony frowned. "Why not? Because I shouldn't let them?"

"Because they can't," George said sadly. "To them, you're not just Tony, you're that black guy, Tony, or their black friend, Tony, or that crazy black guy, Tony, who went berserk at the brook. The color of our skin makes them blind, sometimes. These Belton kids can't see us because they can't get past the blackness." He smiled at Anthony. "Think about your name, son. For real. No matter how many times you tell them, they still keep calling you what they want."

Anthony agreed but then thought about it. Something still didn't make sense to him. "What about you?" Anthony said. "Almost every time I see you, you're hanging out with some white people, laughing and joking around. Seems like you made some friends that really know you."

George smiled. "I did," he said. "It took some work, though. From both sides. I had to drop some stereotypical things associated with black folk."

"Yeah," Anthony joked, "but not basketball, though."

"Not that, but other things," George said. "Things like my music and how loud I listen to it, making sure I pull my pants up and wear a belt. And another thing I don't do is eat fried chicken up here, which is more than I can say about some people. Your girl was at dinner the other night, eating wings like they were going out of style."

At first he wasn't sure, but then Anthony figured it out. "You mean Gloria?"

"The one and only. People like her are dangerous. They can set black people back a hundred years."

"For eating chicken in public? Come on, man," Anthony said. "I don't know about that one."

"How about for being a segregationist, then? I know that she can't stand me for associating with white people. Swear to God, I think she would have been happier during Jim Crow."

"Whatever, man. You just don't know her."

"Yes, I do." George grabbed a paperback from a stack

of books and threw it to Anthony. It was dog-eared and most of the color was worn away, but the title was still legible: *Bury My Heart at Wounded Knee*. "Check it out sometime," George said. "You know that the cowboys scalped the Indians first? When the Native Americans started scalping back, white people started calling them savages."

"That's messed up."

"I know. They also cut the Indians' balls off and used the sacks for tobacco pouches."

Anthony flipped quickly through the yellowed pages, grabbing his crotch while he did so. "So when I read this, I'll understand what you mean about Gloria? 'Cause right now I'm kind of lost."

George sat down and scooted close. "Turn on the TV and what do you see?" he asked. "The Braves, the Redskins, and *your* Cleveland Indians, with that big-toothed clown on the uniform. They took a whole race and made them two-dimensional, just a bunch of drunks and mascots."

"I know," Anthony said, and moved back a little. "Like I said, that's messed up."

"Don't you see, though? Now you got half the Native Americans believing that crap, doing everything they can to fit into that image. What happened to them is the same thing that's happening to black people, only our self-hatred runs so deep that we like to shoot each other." George sniffed. "Gloria is the worst kind of black girl in the world, reinforcing every negative stereotype she can find, always crying racism when something doesn't go her way, intimidating white folks with all that stupid *attitude*. Forget the KKK and the skinheads, son. People like Gloria will put those fools outta business."

Anthony stared for a while and tried to put it all together. George thought Gloria was too black. And Gloria thought George was an Uncle Tom. They saw themselves as opposites, but Anthony disagreed. If they ever took the time to really listen to each other, they would see they weren't very far apart.

Before dinner, Anthony played basketball with a bunch of other varsity hopefuls. His game was still the worst, but he had come a long way since September. George even said so, and the compliment excited everyone except for Khalik, whose court mastery over Anthony was weakening.

Silhouetted in the window high above the floor

was Coach Rockwell, his office lit up behind him. He tapped on the glass and waved.

"Peep it," George said, glancing up. "Coach thinks you might have a chance to be a swinger. Hector did it last season, and look at him now."

"It's the truth, bro," Hector said. "The best of both worlds. Starter on JV and garbage time on varsity. Either way, all I had to do was shoot."

"Then your boy's in trouble," Khalik said, and laughed a little too loudly. "Slow-Hio still can't make a foul shot."

That night, Anthony sat at his desk during study hours, puzzling over the marks on his latest English paper. Gone were the silly spelling mistakes that had plagued him for weeks, corrected were all the problems with grammar and punctuation that MLK Junior High had failed to address. But on the back of the last page, there was still a long-winded comment scrawled in red ink. It said that Anthony had to learn how to dig deeper, that his essays still read like simple reports, lacking passion or original thought. And the grade at the bottom, consistent as always, was a prominently circled C.

Anthony sighed at his roommate, who had his head

in a French book. Brody looked up. "Bonjour, *mangeur*." Brody winked at Anthony. "That means 'hello, eater,' but I like the rhyme."

"I think I'm in trouble," Anthony said, holding up his graded essay. "No matter what, I just can't get this shit right."

"I know what you mean." Brody closed his book and pushed it away. "All this French is Greek to me." They shared a laugh and Brody turned to his computer, put on a song by the Doors, and dialed the sound down low.

Anthony jeered. "Boo! Put on something by that other dude you played for me. Floyd Pinkney."

"You mean Pink Floyd, not Floyd Pinkney. And it's a band, dude. Not a person."

"I don't care, just play it. Maybe it'll help me concentrate."

Mellow music filled the room. Anthony looked at his paper again, balled it up, and threw it in the trash. Then he went through his desk for all his other failures, smashed them up, and tossed them, too. He felt better, but it hadn't changed anything. He would still have to work his ass off to be average.

"Tough day at the office?" Brody had been watching

him the whole time, smiling out of one side of his mouth.

"I don't know why you're laughing. Both of us are gonna end up in the support center. Your grades are as bad as mine."

"You mean sports center," Brody corrected. "Nobody's ever in there but dumb jocks."

Yeah, Anthony thought. Dumb jocks and almost every student of color on campus. So far he had avoided it, but now it seemed inevitable. At least Brody would be there to help blur the color line. "Once they put you in, how long do you have to stay?"

"I dunno," Brody said. "Good question. Maybe for the rest of the year or until you get your grades up, whichever comes first."

Anthony thought of the windowless room in the main building that smelled like feet and mildew. He didn't want to spend two and a half hours in there every night, being bossed around by Mr. Voght. I have to do better, he said to himself, and then settled his eyes on Brody. "I'm serious, we need to get it together. Both of us."

"You sound like my dad," Brody said, leaning back. "'Get it in gear, or get left behind.'" He laughed, but it didn't sound happy. "He's always saying stuff like that, like I have to race against the whole world. . . . Dude, I don't know. Sometimes I just wanna grab a backpack and tool around, playing songs, meeting cool people, never putting down roots. You ever heard of a walk-about? In Australia, some people drop everything and just walk around for weeks, chasing kangaroos and living with nature."

"Sounds like fun."

"It is, dude!" Brody said, missing the sarcasm. "Get up and go to sleep when you feel like it, no road to tell you where to go, nobody's stupid platitudes and bass-ackward rules to follow. Just you, in nature, with no one else around. If that's not getting close to God, then I don't know what is."

"You believe in God?" Anthony asked, growing interested. "I took you for one of those other people."

"An atheist? No, dude, I believe in God. And when She gets back, She's gonna be pissed!" He tapped a lit-tle drumroll on his thighs.

Anthony laughed with him but didn't know what to think. God had to be a man. Otherwise, the world wouldn't be so full of vengeance. "A walkabout, huh?" he said, warming to the idea of it. After all, wasn't that what he did back at home, hanging on the train tracks? "That sounds cool. You saw that in Australia? How long were you there?"

"How about never, dude," Brody said, sounding surprised. "Who can afford to go Australia?"

You can, Anthony thought. You and almost everyone else in the school. "If I could go anywhere, I would wanna go to Africa. Get to see some lions and cheetahs and shit. Plus, I wouldn't be a minority over there," he said, smiling. "In Africa, *you* would be the one everybody noticed."

From the hall came the sounds of doors opening and closing. Study hours were over, and the kids were free. Like clockwork, Brody grabbed his stash and headed toward the door. He asked Anthony if he wanted to come along and, like always, was declined. "Maybe some other time," Anthony said. "Gotta keep my head clear."

Brody left, and Anthony did the same a short time afterward, cruising campus and looking for Gloria, hoping for a chance to casually bump into her. She still didn't know that he liked her, and that was fine with him. Anthony wasn't ready for rejection.

He didn't see her, though, and it was getting cold. He

went back inside and was surprised to find the phone nook empty. On a whim, he called home and spoke to his mother. After a few minutes of teasing and small talk, her voice took on a different tone. "We need to talk about Thanksgiving," she said. "I don't know if we can afford to bring you home."

The next day, Anthony sat in English class, barely listening. The vacation news had haunted him all night. His mother had said she wasn't sure yet, but he could hear it in her voice. No way would she be able to pay all her bills and buy a plane ticket. He wasn't going home, which meant he had to find somewhere else to go.

"So how about it?" Mr. Hawley said from the front of the room. "Steinbeck called it 'the animal,' but it still boils down to mob mentality, just like in the other story."

A hand shot up. It belonged to Alex Sanger. "Somewhat akin to the fog of war," he stated. "Disturb a beehive or an anthill, and the insects respond with crushing force, attacking anything within a certain radius, regardless of guilt or innocence, subspecies or size. Human soldiers are practitioners of that very kind of group think. In times of battle, they can commit atrocities, but the fog, I suspect, exonerates them."

"But those are soldiers," Gloria protested. "Steinbeck was talking about everyday people." She looked at Mr. Hawley. "Are you saying people in mobs aren't responsible for their actions? We can't blame them because they surrendered their will to some animal . . . ? No disrespect, but that's garbage."

"Is it?" another kid asked, clearly affected. Her name was Debbie Callahan, and she was from a town near Lewiston. "Mob mentality started the Revolutionary War. Without that, we would all still be under British rule."

"Yeah, and mob mentality killed a lot of slaves, too," Gloria shot back. "Don't forget about that."

The two girls glowered at each other. Mr. Hawley cleared his throat, but then Alex raised his hand again. "Interesting postulate," Alex said. "History shows that the Brits ended slavery well before we did. If they had won the Revolutionary War, would they have ended slavery on this continent?" He gestured toward Anthony and Gloria. "And if so, would our two most appreciated classmates never have lived here?"

Debbie mumbled something, and the boy next to her laughed.

"What's so funny?" Mr. Hawley asked, growing agitated.

The boy turned red and bit his lip. Then he pointed at Debbie. "Ask her."

"Well?" Mr. Hawley shifted his gaze to Debbie. She pouted and scribbled circles on her notebook. "We're waiting?"

"Nothing," she said not looking up. "Just a stupid joke about all the Salamis in Lewiston. I'm sorry."

"Dude!" Brody said, speaking up for the first time. "Not cool!"

That afternoon before dinner, Anthony found his roommate in bed. Brody had stormed off right after class and stayed invisible. "Where you been all day?"

"Here and there," Brody said absently. "Town. The woods. Wherever." He sat up and shook his head. "Sorry about Debbie, dude. People like her really piss me off."

"Tell me about it." Anthony thought about the word Debbie had used and where he'd heard it before. "Salamis," he said, leaning down on his elbows. "What was that supposed to mean?"

Brody looked surprised. "Somebody from Somalia.

It's kind of a slur, you know, because Muslims don't eat pork." He paused and sat up completely, flipped the hair out of his eyes, and smiled. "Dude, you do know about all the Somalis in Lewiston, right? Like more than anywhere in the state."

"What?" Anthony said, unimpressed. "Four?"

"Try four thousand, dude. Maybe more."

Anthony made a face. "We're talking about black people, right?"

"Yeah, but don't call them that. And whatever you do, don't call them African American, either. That really ticks them off, for some reason."

Anthony smiled. He wasn't going home for Thanksgiving, but maybe he would still see some black people. "I need to ask you a question." He told Brody about his vacation dilemma. "I might still be able to get home, but I needed to know, just in case."

"Sure, dude," Brody said, but he didn't look very sure at all.

On Thanksgiving Day, Anthony sat at a table in Lewiston, watching Brody's father carve up the big bird and wondering what his family was doing at home in East Cleveland. It was after six, which meant they'd already eaten hours ago, and his mother and Aunt Florence were probably getting drunk and complaining about men. And his brothers had already gotten up from their naps, gone outside, and gotten into something.

"Pass your plate, dear."

He handed his dish to Brody's compassionate mother. Her eyes had been filled with pity since the moment that he got there. The way that she treated him made Anthony uncomfortable, like she thought he was an abused orphan. It made Anthony miss home even more. Brody had been right about Lewiston. Black people from Somalia and other places in Africa walked around with kufis or scarves on their heads. A few were dressed like Anthony, but he hadn't connected with any of them. At a thrift store to buy more used bowling shirts, the dark clerk had nearly bowed down to Brody but treated Anthony like he was invisible.

"Here you go, buddy," Mr. Lavallee announced as the plate came back around. Anthony looked at the dry meat and wet stuffing, the neat peas and what he guessed was cranberry sauce. At home, it came clean and in the shape of the can, not riddled with actual berries. "Thank you," he said, and waited for everyone else to get served. Then Brody's father bowed his head, thanked Jesus, and told them all to dig in.

"Bet you don't get a spread like this at home, huh?" the man said, forking food.

Anthony smiled. "No, sir." The spread at home was twice as big. Twice as big and a hundred times easier to eat. "Do you think I could make a phone call after dinner? I haven't talked to my mother yet."

"Of course, dear," Mrs. Lavallee said. "Just dial one. We don't mind paying for it."

"Yeah," her husband added. "As long as it's not to Mogadishu."

She laughed and sawed into her turkey. "Oh, you. Always the kidder."

After dinner, Anthony called home, but no one picked up. Then he went down to the basement, where Brody was playing video games. The house was big, but nowhere as big as Anthony had imagined. If the Lavallees had money, they were hiding it well. "Can I play?"

"You can play," Brody said, motioning toward the other controller. "But can you beat me?"

"Like a baldheaded stepchild."

They raced their cars around oval tracks and

through snowy woods, across deserts, and along mountain passes. Brody won most often, but Anthony took his fair share, until Mr. Lavallee moved in front of the screen.

"Evening, ladies," he said. "Time to stop destroying the universe and help earn some real money." He was in a leather apron and had goggles around his neck. It made Anthony think about Stephen King.

"Where we going?"

Mr. Lavallee laughed, and after a pause, Brody laughed, too. "Someplace cool," his roommate said, and tugged Anthony along. "Nothing to worry about, dude. You'll like it."

They went behind the garage and into a wooden shack with one door and a dirty window. Inside and hanging head up from a hook was a hollowed-out deer with black and glassy eyes.

"Whoa," Anthony said, and took a step back, bumping into Brody's laughing father.

"Don't worry," the man said, and slid on his goggles. "This one ain't gonna bite you." He put on gloves and grabbed a big knife from the wall, cut a circle around the animal's neck, and connected it to the long belly slit. Then he grabbed the skin and started pulling it down, carving it away from the white fat and pink flesh. "Coming to the end of hunting season," Mr. Lavallee said as he worked. "Business is getting backed up."

It was then that Anthony noticed the other carcasses on the floor, already gutted and stacked up in a corner, their straight legs sticking out. "If it wasn't for this," Brody's father continued, "we could never afford Belton. Friggin' immigrants got all the other jobs." He made a final savage cut across the tail, and the pelt came off cleanly.

Brody rolled his eyes, put on gloves, and grabbed a knife. Inside an hour the two of them had cut away the meat, rolled up the pieces in white paper, and set them aside. Anthony was amazed to see his roommate work so skillfully. This Brody was nothing like the slow-moving burnout he knew. When they were done, Mr. Lavallee asked if he wanted to do another one. "You, too, Tony," he said. "You can help me skin it."

"No, thanks, Mr. Lavallee."

"Same here," Brody chimed in, and peeled off his gloves. "I'm supposed to be on vacation."

They sat in front of the TV screen again, this time playing soccer instead of racing cars. Anthony told

Brody about how he'd had to work at the barbershop, how free tuition at Belton hadn't seemed very free at all.

"Dude, I should be on work-study, but my dad won't let me do it." He blew the hair out of his eyes and tapped the controller. "If you haven't already figured it out, he's proud and has a particular view of the world."

"I hear you," Anthony said, and checked behind them. "To tell the truth, I'm surprised he let me stay here. I'm surprised he even let you be my roommate."

"He didn't want me to at first. Thought you were gonna steal all my stuff."

"There's still time," Anthony said, taking a shot at the goal. "I'm just waiting for you to let your guard down."

EIGHT

AFTER VACATION, THEY QUICKLY FELL BACK INTO the Belton groove, only now Anthony spent afternoons trying out for basketball, while Brody attacked the ski slopes. One day a couple of packages arrived for Brody from Lewiston. One was a ski suit, sent by his mother. The other was a lone can of deodorant, in a plain cardboard box.

"Who sent you that?" Anthony asked, laughing at the Right Guard. "Somebody must be trying to tell you something."

"They are," Brody said, and locked the door. "They're saying, 'Smoke up, dude! The bud in Lewiston at harvesttime is a lot to be thankful for.'" Brody picked up the can and unscrewed the bottom. Then he pulled out a plump bag of weed. "Couldn't get it while we were there, so I had it shipped. Care to partake?"

"Okay."

Brody looked at him in surprise as Anthony smiled back, more than a little stunned himself. "Hurry up," he said. "Let's go before I change my mind."

"Give me thirty seconds." Brody shoved into a parka, grabbed what he needed, and led Anthony off into the woods. They found a mossy rock big enough for them to sit on and smoked. The high Anthony got from the little glass pipe was the best he ever had.

"You were right," he said, laughing for no reason. "This really is some good-ass weed."

Brody nodded and then packed the bowl again. He lit it, and they passed it back and forth, smoking easily. "I need to ask you something," Brody said. "How come you never did this with me before?"

"Because I didn't know you before. Now I do."

Brody leaned back. *"Getting to know you, getting to know more about you . . ."* He laughed. "That has to be like the worst song in the world, dude."

"You don't hear me arguing," Anthony said. "Especially when you sing it."

They talked and teased each other a while longer, until Brody stood up and announced that he was hungry. After drops of Visine and mouthfuls of Reese's Pieces, the boys went into town.

In the supermarket, they grabbed Oreos, Nilla Wafers, and potato chips. On their way to the front, Brody picked up a few jars of Gerber baby food.

"Are you serious?"

Brody grinned at the jars in the basket. "I know. Crazy, right? Dude, I just gotta try these sweet potatoes!"

The man at the register looked at them strangely as they unloaded all of their food. "You guys from Belton?" he asked, scanning the items.

"Yeah, dude," Brody said happily. "I'm Brody Peyote and this here's Anthony Epiphany. Pleased to meet your personage."

"You guys are high, huh?" the cashier asked. His name tag said MARK. "Don't worry, I'm not a narc. What do you think I'm gonna do, first thing I get home?"

"That's awesome," Brody said. "Mark's not a narc." The three of them laughed as Brody paid for the food. Then Anthony saw a black man approaching, the first he had seen in Hoover.

He was slender and dressed in a button-down shirt that had MANAGER and AL-SAID stitched above the breast pocket. "Mark?" the man said, walking directly toward them. "When you are finished with these young men, I need you to investigate something. A woman insists that she can buy power tools here, but I know we do not sell these things."

"I'll get right on it. Sir."

Anthony waved, but the manager walked past him and shook Brody's hand. "Hello, young man," he said. "Welcome to the Farmer's Corner. You have enjoyed your shopping?"

Brody nodded, and the manager turned to leave.

"Asshole," Mark hissed as he stuffed the bag. "Goddam illegal immigrant, job-stealing, Salami son of a bitch."

Walking back, Anthony didn't have the munchies anymore. And he didn't feel very high, either. "That's the second time," he said of the manager's snub. "First at that store in Lewiston and now this. What do you think they have against me? I'm just as dark as him, if not darker."

"I dunno," Brody said. "Maybe everybody needs someone to hate."

★ ★ ★

The next evening, Anthony met George in the gym to fine-tune his game. There was only one practice before the coach made the cuts, and Anthony still had an outside chance. Varsity basketball. The thought of it made him work even harder, until George finally called for a timeout. "What got into you?" George asked, sitting down. "Play like that tomorrow and you might take my spot."

"I don't know about that," Anthony said, and suppressed a smile. "But maybe I can start on JV."

Gloria walked in wearing headphones and dribbling a basketball. She saw them and rolled her eyes, went to the far end of the court, and shot lazy jumpers.

"That's my cue," George said, and got to his feet. "You should stick around and handle your business, though, before Paul or somebody else scoops her up."

Anthony grabbed a ball and went to the free-throw line, concentrated on the rim and the sounds from behind him; a few bounces, short silence, and then the swish of the net or, more often, the thud of the ball against the rim. Gloria was good but not incredible, more middle of the pack in the girls' hoop pecking order than anywhere near the top.

He took his shot and missed, chased the ball down, and went back to the line. This time he tried to block out the other sounds, but the bouncing behind him grew closer and louder. A ball came sailing over his head, snapped the net as it fell through the rim. "Game over," Gloria said, trotting by to retrieve it. "Think you can do that?"

"Easy." Anthony stepped behind the three-point arc, flicked his wrist, and by some miracle the ball went in. "What I tell you? Piece of cake."

"Scared of you," she said, laughing. "Guess all that work is paying off. Maybe Uncle Tom is good for something after all."

"Leave George alone," he said. "The dude is all right. You just don't know him."

"I know enough." Gloria sniffed. "I know brothers like him are dangerous."

"There you go again," Anthony said, at first faking the frustration but then realizing that it was genuine. "Why do you always have to put him down? Call him names just because he has a lot of friends? White people can be good, too. You can't lump them all in one box."

"Why can't I? They do it to us." She looked at him

with sad eyes and wedged her ball underneath an arm. "Oh, no," she said. "Don't tell me you're about to run out here and start chasing white girls, too?"

"I'm in Maine," Anthony said, "at an all-white prep school. Who else am I supposed to chase?"

Gloria smiled then and slid her headphones back on. "I don't know," she said, walking toward the exit. "But not every girl in this school is white."

Anthony didn't make the varsity team, and it couldn't have bothered him less. Gloria liked him, or at least she was interested, and that was all that really mattered. The two of them were in town one day when they ran into Brody and Venus. It was cold, and Venus was wearing a hood, but a gust of wind blew it off.

Gloria leaned closer to Anthony and whispered, *"Oh. My. God."* Venus had twisted her hair into flat and dirty dreadlocks. "Is she serious?"

"You dudes wanna stop somewhere before we get back to campus?" Brody asked, patting his pocket. "Got some of Lewiston's finest, right here."

"That's okay, man. Some other time."

"Yeah," Gloria said coldly. "Some other time." She was still locked in on the hair.

Venus ran a hand through her new tangle and smiled proudly. "It's really cool, right?" she said. "It took me forever. I don't know how you do it."

"Do what?" Gloria snapped. "Does it look like I have any dreadlocks?"

Venus blushed. "Sorry. I just meant . . . you know. Black people."

Anthony gently held her arm, but Gloria twisted free. "Of course I know what you mean," she said, and showed her front teeth. "Come here. Let me look at it." Venus bowed, and Gloria lifted one of the clumps. "Ooh, yeah," she continued. "I really like this. What did you use?"

"Mostly beeswax and a few other things," Venus said. "I heard real dreadlocks use cow dung, but I'm not gonna find that around here."

"Cow dung?" Anthony made a face. "Who the hell would—" Gloria shot him a look and he stopped. Then she turned her attention back to the blond girl.

"I'm sure you can find some," Gloria said. "I'll even help you out, if you want me to."

Venus blushed again. "Wow. That's awesome."

On campus, the couples separated. Gloria was still fuming, and although he understood why she was so upset, a part of Anthony thought she was overreacting. So what if the girl had tried an African hairstyle? If anything, she had done it to show solidarity, not as a sign of disrespect.

But maybe that was only big George speaking in his mind, telling Anthony to give up more ground in the invisible war to win nothing.

"You okay?"

Gloria had covered her face with both hands. "No," she said. "Are you?"

Anthony nodded. "Yeah, I'm straight. No big deal, to me."

"Then I feel sorry for you." She scooted away from him. "Suzy Cream-cheese wearing dreadlocks . . . I don't know how you can be friends with her ignorant ass."

"She's not my friend," Anthony said. "And she's not my enemy, either. She's Brody's burnout girlfriend. That's all." He put a hand on her back, but she jerked away. She was beautiful, but anger made her ugly sometimes. "You want me to go?"

"Do what you want. I don't care."

"Do what I want to?"

"You heard me."

Before he could think about it, Anthony gently knocked the hands away from her face and kissed her. It was just as warm and soft as he'd imagined. "You said to do what I wanted," he said, stealing a glance at her.

She touched his arm. "About time. I was starting to call you *Slow*-hio for real."

They met in the gym after study hours and kissed until it was time to go to their dorms. Just before going inside, though, Gloria nearly broke Anthony's heart. "We need to slow down," she said. "I'm really not looking for a boyfriend right now."

Anthony stared. "Are you serious?"

"Don't look like that," she said, and touched his face. "I said slow down, not stop hanging out."

On the way to his dorm, Anthony thought about all the times he'd used similar lines on girls at home. Girls he'd fooled around with but didn't really like. But if Gloria wasn't interested, then why had she flirted with him in the first place? Why had she said "about time" and kissed him for half the night? Maybe it was all the kissing that had made her change her mind. He wasn't tall, and she was probably tired of bending down.

Brody was already in the room when he got there, lying on his bed and reading a guitar magazine. "Smells like farts in here," Anthony grumbled, walking by to open a window. "How can you even breathe?"

Brody grunted and turned a page. "Sorry. I was alone when it happened."

"Well, you ain't alone now." He dropped down at his desk and blindly grabbed a book; tried to read but couldn't concentrate. From the corner of his eye, he saw Brody roll over and sit up. Then he dropped his magazine on the floor and loudly cleared his throat.

"So, Tony Romeo," he said. "Saw you and Gloria in a serious lip-lock. Dude, you must be psyched!"

"Something like that." Anthony thought about her parting words. "Why do girls always have to make things so mysterious? Why can't they just say exactly what they mean?"

"Because that would spoil their fun."

"I'm serious, man." Anthony told him what Gloria had said at the end of their night. Then he looked at his roommate and waited.

"Wow," Brody said finally. "I have no idea what that means."

"Me neither. That's the problem. Tomorrow I'm just

gonna ask her, flat out."

Brody flipped the hair out of his eyes and shook his head. "Not tomorrow, dude. Too soon. Sometimes girls don't say what they mean because they don't really know what they want."

Anthony opened his mouth but didn't say anything. His roommate was smarter than he looked. Not once had he even stopped to consider that Gloria was just telling the truth. "So how long should I wait?"

"Don't ask me. I'm making this up as I go along. . . . *Just a song, sung by a humble Brody bard, without a shard of* . . . shit. Dude, that really sucked." He laughed, and Anthony laughed with him. And he thought about Mookie, like he always did whenever Brody made up a song. He missed home, but he was also really beginning to like Belton. Despite all the rules, it didn't feel like prison anymore.

"I had a friend who could do that," Anthony said. "He rapped, but it was the same thing, making up lyrics on the spot. He was pretty good sometimes. Just like you."

Brody bowed. The hair fell back in front of his eyes and stayed there. "Why, thank you, kind sir. Maybe me and your friend could do a little duo sometime."

"I don't think so," Anthony said, and then stopped himself. He hadn't told anyone at Belton about Mookie. Not even the kids from Brooklyn.

"Why not?" Brody asked, laughing. "Afraid we might be a big success, make a ton of cash, and go Hollywood?"

"He got shot. Somebody killed him." Anthony had trouble with it at first, but he told Brody the whole story, and how the murder had scared him all the way to Maine.

Brody listened silently until it was finished. "Sorry, man."

"You don't need to apologize," Anthony said. "I saw the dude who did it, and he didn't look like you."

NINE

FOR THE REST OF THE DAYS UNTIL CHRISTMAS
vacation, Anthony thought more and more about
home. He was excited about seeing his family and
friends, but he was also afraid. He'd been gone almost
four months. What if he had changed too much? What
if he didn't fit in anymore? What if he was going home
to be murdered, just like Mookie?

The questions stayed with him on the van ride to
Portland, and they grew more intense on his flights.
But when the plane touched down in Cleveland and he
saw his beaming mother, Anthony pushed the questions out of his mind and ran to her. They almost fell
down as they crushed each other and rocked from side

to side. He couldn't believe how short she was and how small she felt in his arms.

"Look at you!" she said, pushing away and gawking. "You done got so big, boy. What they feeding you?"

"Noodles and cottage cheese." He laughed, and she slapped his chest. "Seriously, though," he said, "the food is good. And they feed me a lot of it, too."

She seemed to wince, but it passed so quickly that Anthony wasn't sure. "Is that the only bag you brought?"

He shook his head and switched the Belton book bag to his other shoulder. He had charged it to his school account without asking her permission. "Brought that brown suitcase, too."

"Well, hurry up and get it so we can go," she said, looking around. "These airports be making me nervous."

They took the Eddy Road exit off the highway, turned away from all of Bratenahl's mansions, and drove toward East Cleveland's check-cashing joints, beverage stores, and bars. There were broken bottles on the sidewalks and shattered safety glass at the curbs, forsaken houses with busted furniture rotting on their weedy lawns. Massive Navigators floated down the roads on chrome rims, while other cars in far worse shape sputtered along. And every few corners, groups of menacing boys laughed like they owned the world.

"Can you speed up?"

His mother checked the dashboard and frowned. "I'm doing the limit right now. You don't wanna get pulled over, do you?"

"Not around here," he mumbled. "What's with all the empty houses?"

"People cain't make they payments no more, baby. It's a miracle we still got a place to stay."

They pulled into the driveway, and memory flooded him; the cracked concrete slab that had once been a garage; the little patch of yard that he used to think was big; the railroad tracks rising beyond the back fence; and the hole in the links that was his.

"Welcome home, baby," his mother said, and opened the door. Anthony's heart sank when no one yelled out, "Surprise!"

"Where is everybody?"

"I don't know," his mother said. "Somewhere." She scratched her head and then kissed his, said that she had to get up early for work, went in her room, and closed the door.

Anthony walked from room to room, touching things and trying to get comfortable. It all looked familiar but felt different somehow, like he was in another dimension. He called Floyd, but no one answered at his house and his cell number wasn't working. He tried Reggie, but his brother said he was already drunk and passed out for the night. Anthony hung up and thought of other numbers to call, but he went up the stairs instead.

The next evening, Anthony caught up with his friends. They were down in Reggie's basement, drinking and smoking, playing video games. He had stopped by the beverage store on his way over, picked up a six-pack from the uncaring Arab behind the bulletproof glass. His friends cracked up when they saw the Sam Adams, though. It made him wish he had come empty-handed.

"This nigga done brought white boy brews," Floyd said, laughing. "Is that what they got you drinking up there?" He stopped the game and reached for the big bottle between his feet. "Here you go, nigga, drink this eight ball."

Anthony took the malt liquor and unscrewed the top, took a deep swig from the forty-ounce bottle, and wiped his mouth. It was flat and tasted like rusty nails and sugar, but he took another swallow, anyway. "Now that's good brew," he announced, and passed the bottle on. "I don't know the last time I had some Olde E."

Floyd started the game up again. Then he promptly shot Reggie's crouching character through the head. "Next!" He put down the controller and waited but no one made a move. "What about you, Ant? Feel like gettin' shot?"

"Not me, son. I don't even know what game that is."

Floyd frowned and cocked his head to the side just as Reggie sparked a blunt. He hit it and ashed it, then hit it again, blew long clouds from his nostrils, and extended his hand. "Here you go, nigga. Or maybe you don't smoke weed no more, neither?"

"Ant stopped blazing?" Curtis shouted from the other side of the room. "What's wrong? They be testing your piss up there?"

"Hell yeah, they be doing that," Reggie answered. "White people be using that technology." Everyone agreed. There were cameras on RTA trains and buses, plus more posted high up on telephone poles. "Everywhere a nigga go nowadays, it be somebody shooting video."

They all nodded again and moved a little closer to Anthony, either to watch him hit the weed or to take it away. He put it to his lips and took in the ragged smoke, felt like coughing but willed himself not to. Smoking with Brody, there hadn't been any tobacco to deal with.

"Satisfied?"

"For now, nigga," Floyd said, reaching for the blunt. "But the night is young, ain't no school tomorrow, and the weed man is sitting right here." He pulled a pouch from under his seat and dumped out dozens of little Ziploc bags. Each one had a skull and crossbones stamped on the side and was stuffed with green buds of marijuana. "You like them sacks, right?"

As if to answer, Curtis came over and handed him four fives. Floyd added the cash to a wad in his sock and then gave him the fattest bag. "So tell niggas about Maine," he said, leaning in toward Anthony. "I know it gotta be wild."

"Like college," Reggie answered before Anthony could. "They be having keg parties and the whole nine."

"No, they don't, son," Anthony said. "Stop frontin' like you know how it is."

"Yeah, *son*," Floyd said, laughing. "Stop *fronting*." He pulled a bottle from Anthony's six-pack and opened it. "Is that how they got you talking up there?" He laughed again and took a sip, looked surprised, and nodded at the bottle. "This white-boy brew ain't that bad. . . . You won't never catch me buying this shit. But I can drink it."

"That's what's up," Reggie agreed, and opened one for himself. His brother did the same and then Anthony followed.

"So what's the deal, dawg?" Floyd continued while he rolled another blunt. "You gon' tell us about that school or what?"

"I can tell yaw," Anthony said, measuring his words. He had worried so much about not sounding white that he had talked like the Brooklyn kids instead. "But like I already told you on the phone, it's boring."

Reggie laughed and said, "So what, *son*? I wanna know what other words you done learned up there."

"And the bitches, too," Curtis interrupted. "I heard them white girls is freaks."

They waited, and then Anthony told them about his roommate, the other students, and the campus. He told them what happened at Freshman Brook, about his trip to Lewiston and all the Africans he saw. He spun everything in a way that made the experience seem horrible, even though he really was starting to like Belton a lot.

"Damn, nigga," Reggie said, and handed Ant the blunt. "Glad I ain't had to go up there to that bullshit school."

The night wore on, and Anthony slowly faded from the dialogue. There were stories with people's names that he barely recognized, references to things and places that sounded foreign. Just four months away, and his memory was already fuzzy. What would it be like for him after four years?

Anthony needed a present for Gloria, so on Christmas Eve, he took the train downtown to Tower City. It felt good to be in a crowd of mixed people, and Anthony slowed his pace while everyone else rushed around. Some of the shoppers looked like teachers at Belton or like some of the old codgers in Hoover. They walked alone or together, carrying boxes and bags, talking into cell phones or to each other. Packs of teenagers moved in and out of the stores, too. Some groups were as black as Anthony and others as white as Brody.

Although they sometimes passed very close to one another, they never talked or touched. How many times had he come down there before and done the same thing? How many times had he snubbed potential friends?

Anthony smiled at a blond girl. She didn't see him, though, and kept talking to her buddy. A group of girls at another table only glared when he spoke to them, and a boy who looked like Nate stared straight ahead. At first Anthony got mad. Then he noticed his hooded sweatshirt, baggy jeans, and untied Timberlands. If he'd been wearing his acceptable academy clothes, they probably would have treated him differently.

He bought Gloria a necklace and a box of Godiva chocolates. Then he hurried down the stairs and jumped into a waiting Rapid. The last handful of white people got out of the train at University Circle, including the driver, who was replaced by a black woman.

They reached the end of the line in East Cleveland. Anthony walked away from the station, boxed necklace stuffed in his waistband, candy in a bag and swinging at his side. He had probably gone overboard with the gifts for Gloria. They had kissed and hugged a few more times, but she still didn't consider them a couple.

Maybe he would keep the cheap chain to himself. It would probably turn her neck green, anyway.

By the time he reached Hayden Avenue, all of the streetlights were on. Traffic passed by slowly, and Anthony waited for the light to change. Then a dented car suddenly accelerated and yanked up on the sidewalk in front of him. Four doors opened up and five boys hustled out, all of them wearing red baseball caps. "W'sup, nigga?" the biggest one barked. "Ready to pop some more shit?"

Anthony looked at him and then at all the other boys. He had never seen any of them before. "No disrespect, man," Anthony said carefully. "I don't know what you're talking about."

"Yeah, he do!" one of the other ones shouted. "Go 'head and fuck that nigga up, Chop!"

The big one balled his fists, and Anthony dropped the bag. If he ran, they would chase him down. If he stayed and fought, they would all jump on him, anyway. The most that he could hope for was that none of them had a gun. If that was the case, then everything was over. "I'm telling you, dawg," Anthony said, backing up. "You got me confused."

"Hold up, Chop," one of the boys said, moving closer.

"This ain't him. The nigga we lookin' for is way taller."

"Yeah," someone else said from the back. "The other nigga wasn't that black, neither,"

They piled into the car and peeled off. Anthony took a deep breath and picked up his bag. People around him either drove or walked the street, oblivious to what had just almost happened.

He found his mother in the kitchen, cooking. Christmas Day meant a Thanksgiving-sized meal but rarely a tree or presents. Santa Claus was for children, his mother had explained, and she considered Anthony a young man.

She looked up from the stove and at the bag in his hand, raised her eyebrows, and asked, "Who is that for?" Instead of telling the truth, Anthony smiled and extended it. Gloria wasn't his girlfriend, anyway. "Thank you, baby," she said, and set the candy aside. "But you know I didn't get you anything."

"That's okay. I just wanted you to have it. Sweets for the sweetest mother in the world." She smiled, but it didn't last very long. Disappointed, Anthony searched for something else to say. "Up at school, we did this Secret Santa thing. Everybody in the dorm picked each other's name out of a hat and then we had to buy that person a present." He paused as she went and got something out of the refrigerator. When she returned, he started up again. "Anyway, there was a ten-dollar limit on everything. That way nobody went broke."

"That's nice, baby," she said, stuffing the turkey. "What did you get?"

"A Nerf basketball hoop. I put it on top of my garbage can. Anyway, what I'm saying is that we could probably do it here, in the house, if we wanted to. We wouldn't even have to say it came from Santa Claus." He waited, but his mother didn't look up or say a word. "Why not?"

"'Cause I ain't got money for no bullshit holiday," she snapped. "That's why."

"But ten dollars, Ma? Come on. You spend two or three times that every week, burning gas to go see your boy."

She pulled her hand out from the turkey's ass and wiped it with a rag. "My what?"

"I'm sorry. Your boy*friend*. How is old Patrick, anyway? I haven't seen him around."

She pointed a stiff finger. Lumpy stuffing clung to the nail and knuckles. "Watch yourself, hear? Who I spend my time with ain't none of your business. And since you wanna talk about where my money be going, let's start off with you. How much you think that plane ticket cost? And what about that fancy book bag? You get that for free?"

"No."

"No, what?"

"No, ma'am."

"That's better," she said. "I don't know what they done did to you up there, but I don't like it. You got a smart-ass mouth, all the sudden."

He drew a breath but held it. There was no use in arguing. He did have a smart-ass mouth now, and smart eyes and everything else. "I'm sorry."

"You should be." She jammed in another handful of stuffing. "If all you gon' learn up there is how to act disrespectful, then I'm gon' make your black ass stay here." She sniffed, and then the bird got a final violent treatment. After that, she slid it into the oven.

"Please don't," he said before he could stop himself.

His mother looked up, surprised and wounded at the same time. She washed her hands and then forced a smile. "So you don't like being home no more?"

"It's not like that, Ma. Stop tripping." He told her what had happened on his way back from downtown, how everything and everyone seemed more menacing than before. If he had to come back to East Cleveland now, he would spend all of his time in the house.

She tried to smile again, but it collapsed. Then she rubbed his head and looked at him. "It's bad, Anthony. I don't know what to tell you. But it ain't no worse out there now than it was before you left. Think about what happened to your friend."

"I do," he said. "Every second that I'm here. That's why I can't wait to leave."

On New Year's Eve, Anthony stood in Reggie's back-yard with the rest of his friends, holding a plastic cup of champagne and waiting for midnight, while Floyd slid bullets into the clip. There were ten minutes before the celebration, but successive explosions came from a few houses down. "Damn!" Curtis said, look-ing out over the fences. "Sound like Mr. Thompson got another cannon."

They all laughed and Anthony made sure to laugh with them, and he tried not to think about all those lit-tle cannonballs screaming back down. He wasn't sure who had started the practice of shooting at midnight; all he knew was that his mother used to make them sleep in the basement on the holiday, where it was safe.

"I heard a preacher caught a bad one last year," Anthony said. "Dude had just told the congregation to bow their heads and then a bullet came through the wall."

"Guess it was his time," Reggie said matter-of-factly. "The Lord giveth and He taketh away." He tried to make the sign of the cross on his chest, but he looked more like a baseball manager giving signs. There was a *click* as Floyd slid the clip into the nine millimeter, and then Reggie forgot about what he was doing. "Lemme hold it."

"Eat a dick, nigga," Floyd said. "I'm goin' first."

Reggie called second and then Curtis after him. That left Anthony last, but he didn't care. There was a whisper and a flash as someone lit a blunt.

"Y'all got loot?" Floyd whispered, holding out a wad of cash. It was considered bad luck to start a new year with empty pockets. One by one, they grabbed a bill, knowing that in just a few minutes they would have to give it back. Someone called out Mookie's name and then the names of others who hadn't survived the year. They poured champagne on the ground in their honor, and then the shooting started, all at once and from everywhere. There were shotguns and magnums and automatic MAC-10s, Uzis, and AKs and calibers they couldn't recognize.

Floyd joined the celebration by squeezing shots. Sparks and flame jumped out of the barrel and lit his snarling face. "Happy New Year, trick-ass muh'fuckas!" He popped off a few more and then passed the gun. After that the other two boys took their turns, adding bullets and curses to the sky. But when the pistol finally found its way to Anthony, the slide was open and the clip was empty. "Might as well give it up, dawg," Floyd said with a shrug. "I ain't got no more bullets."

TEN

ANTHONY HAD A DREAM ON HIS FIRST NIGHT HE
returned from vacation. He was older and in a business suit, walking toward his house in East Cleveland and swinging a briefcase. A crowd of young boys on bicycles suddenly filled the street and sidewalk. All were dressed in red and staring at him hard. One of them flashed metal and Anthony tried to run, but when he saw his best friend holding the gun, he couldn't move at all.

"Floyd?"

He worked hard over the next several weeks, and his grades got better. Brody saw the change and even made a big one of his own: He went to smoking weed on weekends only. But it wasn't just in the classroom that Anthony applied himself. He joined study groups, ate his meals at different tables, learned more names and hometowns and hobbies. He even signed up for pottery to fulfill his art elective and befriended kids who didn't eat meat. Seth McCarthy lost his swagger and eventually stopped chasing freshmen around. Some of his classmates thanked Anthony for it, but most didn't make the connection. And all the while, he still pined after Gloria, but she was becoming more distant, not just from Anthony but from the whole school. There were rumors that she wasn't returning in the fall, but he could never get her to talk about it.

One day Anthony was sitting in George's room, listening to one of the big junior's music mixes and reading a copy of *Sporting News*. That night there would be a game against Overlook Academy, and their star player's picture and stats took up an entire magazine page. His name was Tavares Slayton, and he was being heavily recruited by Duke, North Carolina, and Boston College.

"Damn," Anthony said, and put the magazine down. "This dude sounds like Superman."

George shrugged. "He is. Dude average something like twenty-eight and twelve boards. They blow us out every time we play."

"Not this year, though," Anthony said.

George hesitated, and Anthony recognized the look. "So, anyway," he said, and clapped George on his back. "I've been taking your advice, man. Got friends all over the place now." Anthony told him about how he'd gone skiing with Chris and to an Aerosmith concert with other kids. "Thanks for helping me out, man. For real. Otherwise, I don't think I would have lasted this long."

George nodded, but his face was drawn. Later that night, Anthony understood why. Not only did Overlook beat the team in a blowout, their star player held George to nine points.

Winter Carnival came a few weeks later, a day off from classes for contests and games, followed by a talent show that night. Coach Rockwell took the stage after the last act and brought the varsity basketball team with him. They needed to raise money for new warm-ups and were auctioning off their services.

"So how about it, people?" Rockwell boomed into the microphone. "You gonna help these boys look good for the tournament, or what?"

The crowd cheered, and then the coach pulled a big kid from the line. The opening bid was five dollars, but it eventually swelled to thirty. "Is that it?" Rockwell said after the bidding had slowed. "This particular athlete is a gentleman and a scholar. He can pull out your chair and do your homework, too."

The boy nodded, and more hands flew up. He had one of the highest grade-point averages in the school. A girl eventually won him for sixty dollars, and then the coach called the next player. Everyone cheered, and the mood in the auditorium that night grew as bright as the snow outside.

Not for Anthony, though. His mood was dark and getting darker. It had everything to do with the raucous scene on stage and the bitter words from the girl sitting next to him.

"Can you believe this shit?" Gloria asked again. And, like before, she didn't give him time to answer. "Got them up there in an auction. A SLAVE auction!"

A few of the kids around them stared, and Anthony grinned self-consciously. "I hear you," he whispered. "But chill."

"You chill," she said, and crossed her arms. "Got

black people up there, on the auction block . . ."

And white people, too, Anthony thought. But he was smart enough not to say it.

Khalik was the next one to take center stage, and he was greeted by laughter and jeers. The coach tried to open the bidding at five, but the most he could get was three dollars.

"Come on, people," Rockwell implored. Sweat popped on his forehead in beads, and he tightened his grip on the microphone. "Three lousy bucks? You can do better than that. Look at him, he's a sensitive guy. You're liable to hurt this poor boy's feelings."

Going along, Khalik rubbed his eyes with the sides of his fists and pouted. "See what I mean?" Rockwell continued as everyone laughed. "Come on, people. It's for a good cause."

A few hands went up reluctantly, and Khalik was sold for eleven dollars. After that, Coach Rockwell cleared his throat and raised a hand in the air behind him. "And now, people . . . now, what you've been waiting for . . ."

The place erupted as George jumped to the front of the stage, pulled off his Belton sweatshirt, and flexed. People shouted bids from every row in the auditorium, and the price for the big junior multiplied.

"See what I mean?" Gloria snapped. "That's *your* boy up there, half naked. Not mine." She left and Anthony followed close behind, looking for a way to console her. She was right, though. It was fucked up. If George was too blinded to see how he looked, then what did it say about all his advice?

"I hate this place!" she shouted. "You hear me? I hate this fucking place and I wanna go home!"

He tried to hold her, but she pulled away. "I'm going straight to the headmaster about this bullshit and so should you. This school hollers all day about diversity and then goes and has a slave auction. What kind of sense does that make?"

Anthony stammered and said he didn't know. "Maybe they thought it was okay since they had white boys up there, too."

"Yeah, and maybe they didn't think at all." She shook her head. "Never mind. I forgot who I was talking to."

"What's that supposed to mean?"

"I don't know, Anthony. Or Tony, or whatever you let these people call you. You tell me."

Pandemonium broke out from inside the auditorium. George had evidently just been sold.

"I ain't trying to be like him," Anthony said. "Not anymore."

She looked him up and down and said, "It might already be too late. Whose coat is that? Your room-mate's?"

"Yeah. So what?"

"My father always says this thing," she said. "Some-thing like 'Show me three of your friends, and I'll tell you who you are.'" She put her hands on his shoulders. "I like you, Anthony. I really do. But we wouldn't make a good couple. You know that, right?"

He knew. But he didn't want to say it. "You serious about going to Dr. Dirk? What if it backfires? What if we wind up getting in trouble for it?"

"In trouble with who? We weren't the ones selling black people on stage. We're just making a complaint about it."

And that's the problem, Anthony thought. Half the school already saw him as violent; he didn't want to be labeled a militant, too. "Then we shouldn't go together," he said. "Two different people, two differ-ent complaints about the same thing. It'll make our case seem that much stronger."

The next day, Anthony went to see the headmaster.

His office was huge and lined with crowded bookshelves. "Good to see you, Tony," the grinning man said. "Have a seat."

Anthony found the nearest chair and sat down. Dr. Dirk sat behind his desk. "So, how is everything?" the man asked. "Enough snow for you?" He laughed, and Anthony laughed with him.

"It is a lot," Anthony said. "I've never seen this much at one time in my life."

The headmaster laughed again. "Not like New York, right? They never keep a lot of snow on the ground." He winked and then clasped his hands behind his head. "Anyway, Tony. What can I do for you?"

"It's about Winter Carnival," Anthony blurted, to stop himself from correcting the man on his name and hometown. "What Mr. Rockwell did with the team."

"You mean the auction?"

"Yeah, the auction," Anthony continued. "I'm pretty sure he didn't mean anything by it, but with almost every black person in the school being up there for sale, well, in a way it looked kind of racist."

The Headmaster jerked at the mention of the word, but his expression didn't change. "I see," he said. "You think it looked like a slave auction?"

Anthony nodded. "Yes, sir."

"Even with the white kids up there and the fun envi-ronment . . . ? Even though it raised money for a good cause?" Anthony nodded after each question. "Let me ask you something." Dr. Dirk rested his elbows on the desk and leaned in. "Why didn't George Fuller or any of the other black kids on the team say anything about it? If it was racist, why would they even participate?"

Because they were getting new warm-ups, Anthony thought. Because sometimes it was easier to row the boat instead of rock it. "I don't know," he finally answered. "Maybe they did it for the team."

Dr. Dirk took off his glasses and cleaned them with a white cloth. "Would have to be a pretty important team for him to ignore something like that," he said. "I think I'll ask George about it. See what he says."

Anthony slumped. A heart-to-heart between George and the headmaster wasn't going to win him any points with Gloria. "Okay, but I still think the auction was a bad idea, Dr. Dirk. Maybe you should think of doing something different next year, like selling tick-ets to a dance."

Dr. Dirk put his glasses back on and looked at Anthony like he was seeing him for the first time.

"That's an excellent idea," he said. "What year are you, Tony? A freshman, right?"

Anthony nodded. "Yes, sir."

"It takes a lot of guts for a ninth grader to come in here like you did. Especially considering the subject matter. Ever think about student government? I think you'd be a great class representative."

"No, sir," Anthony said. "But Mr. Hawley said something about being a proctor for him next year. I might try that."

"Good. I can see why Mr. Hawley would want you on his floor. You're a natural leader, Tony." He cleaned his glasses again. "You would have to apply, though," he cautioned. "It would mean writing an essay and giving a speech in front of the graduating class, their families, the teachers and trustees . . . think you're up for it?"

"I don't know," Anthony said. "I never wrote a speech before."

"They're easy. I give speeches every day. Just speak clearly, establish eye contact, and be sure to know your subject. And it's always good to sprinkle in a joke or two, for good measure."

"Okay. I'll think about it."

"You should," Dr. Dirk said seriously. "Being a proctor at Belton is a very big deal. You'd be more than just an authority figure. You'd be an extension of the school's proud traditions and history. Trust me, Tony. You want to do this."

Anthony thought about Zach stomping up and down the hall and giving orders, intimidating the freshman boys who were too small to defend themselves or too meek to realize that they should. Was that what the headmaster meant by being an extension of the school? Was sacrificing ninth graders to people like McCarthy supposed to be a proud tradition? He guessed it was, but Anthony didn't think that it should be.

"I'll try," Anthony said finally.

Dr. Dirk rubbed his hands together. "Excellent. Glad to hear it. And as for that other thing, I just want you to know that we take diversity very seriously here. You're not the only student to express concern about the auction, and I promise to investigate it thoroughly."

Anthony bit the inside of his cheek, but the name escaped his mouth anyway. "Gloria?"

The headmaster looked at him over the top of his glasses, drummed his fingers on the desk, and sighed. "Well . . . I think it might be better not to mention individual names," Dr. Dirk said. "It could prove counter to what we are trying to achieve."

Anthony blinked. Achieve what? "Okay," he said. "No names."

"Good!" The headmaster stood up and shook Anthony's hand. "I'm genuinely interested in your perspective on things, Tony. Like, are we doing enough for our minority students?"

Anthony thought. "Well, I think we sho—"

"Not right now," Dr. Dirk said, already moving to the door. "I have a meeting. But you work on that speech and earn that position, Tony. Then we'll have plenty of time to talk."

That afternoon, Anthony went into town alone, walked into the pizza place, and kicked the snow off his feet. Two bearded men in plaid jackets were talking with the woman at the counter. They looked at Anthony, and one of them said, "Speak of the devil."

"Not him," the woman said. "This is one of them New York imports, from that school." She winked at Anthony. "Take your order?"

"Medium pizza, with everything." He paid and slid into an empty booth. Other than the two men at the counter and a few townies playing pool in the back, the place was dead.

"I hear Lisbon Street looks just like Mogadishu," one of the men said. "Mosques and friggin' bazaars everywhere."

"Ayuh," said the other one. "Another bunch of 'em just moved in, up to Birch Street. Won't be long before we get a ghetto, right here . . ."

Anthony moved to a booth in the back, near the pool tables. He knew that the men at the counter were talking about Lewiston, and probably the supermarket manager. Lately everything seemed to be about race: George and Gloria, in his classes, and even with Dr. Dirk. He was tired and wanted to get away from it somehow. But he couldn't, without losing his skin.

More people arrived and ordered food. Anthony was relieved when one of them put money in the jukebox. The woman brought his food, and by the time he finished eating, Brody and Venus showed up. Nate was with them, and they convinced Anthony to shoot a game of pool.

They racked the balls and Nate got ready to break, just as someone at the next table shouted, "Nigger nuts!"

"What the fuck?" Anthony spun around. The one

who had yelled was twice his size.

"I missed a shot," the man said unapologetically. "Don't go civil rights on me." He had a gold crown and halo tattooed on his arm, the same as all the other men with him. The idea of finding a gang in Maine had never crossed Anthony's mind.

"Let's go," Anthony said, pushing past his mute friends. "Before somebody gets hurt."

Walking back, Anthony shared his gang theory. Nate and Venus hadn't noticed the tattoos, but Brody said that he had. "What's up?" Anthony asked. "Is it a gang?"

Brody shrugged. "Not really . . ." He glanced around but not at his friends.

"Not really, but . . . ?" Anthony prodded. "Spit it out."

"I don't know. My dad knows some guys with the same crap on their arm . . . they're all pretty racist, but not a gang." He shrugged again and looked at Anthony. "Sorry, dude."

"For what? You can't pick your father's friends." Or your father, either, Anthony thought. Brody was white, but he wasn't rich. He was smart, but nowhere near Einstein. And although his dad hung with rednecks and racists, Brody would never be like him.

Belton had made sure of that, by having the two

boys live together. It forced them to respect each other. Anthony felt a sudden burst of pride. Not knowing what to do with it, he tripped his roommate and ran.

In the gym a week later, Paul and Khalik played one on one while Anthony sat in the courtside bleachers with Gloria. They'd been talking about movies and other safe topics when Gloria took Anthony's hand. "Why do you let people call you Tony, if that's not your name?"

He shrugged. "I don't know. Guess I got tired of correcting everybody all the time."

"And how's that going for you?"

Laughter from the court drew their attention. The ball was wedged between the backboard and rim, and Khalik was trying to jump up and get it. "Oh my God, boy!" Gloria yelled. "You look like a fat little penguin, trying to fly!"

Anthony smiled, but her question still stung. How *was* it going for him? After seeing his mentor on stage and for sale, shirtless and baring his teeth, Anthony had deliberately gone the other way whenever he caught sight of him. He didn't feel George was an Uncle Tom, but more like a chameleon. Was that bad? Anthony didn't know. Both George and the lizard were kind of fake, but it was how they survived.

"So what's your next move?" Anthony asked. "You know, with Dr. Dirk and what happened at the auction?"

"Do I have one?" Gloria stabbed a finger at the boys on the court. "As long as they don't have a problem with it, the school won't have one, either."

Anthony nodded. "That's why I'm trying to be a proctor next year. Get a foot in the door and change things from the inside."

"Well, good luck with that one," she said. "I won't be around here to see it, but good luck anyway."

He watched Paul and Khalik. They would be back at school next year. So would Brody and Venus. So would George. But not Gloria. "You know, you and George are kind of the same," Anthony said. "He runs away from himself by trying to please everybody and you, you're just running away."

He left after that and wandered campus, lost track of time and was late for in-dorms. Mr. Voght was on duty and unlocked the front door. But he didn't let Anthony pass. "What is it with you guys? You're late?"

"I know. Sorry."

Voght looked surprised. "That's it? No jive about

being down in the gym? No 'Come on, Mr. Voght, man, you know how it *ee-is*?'" Voght chuckled and stepped to the side.

"That's racist," Anthony said, walking by him. "Just thought you might like to know."

Voght stopped him. "Now, wait a minute," he said, clearly disturbed by the comment. "I don't have a racist bone in my body. When you were still just a gleam in your daddy's eye, I was halfway around the world, risking my life for yellow people."

Anthony went downstairs and bumped into Mr. Hawley, doing his rounds. "Hey, Tony," he asked pleasantly. "How's it hanging?"

Instead of answering, Anthony clenched his teeth.

"Want to talk about it?"

Anthony didn't, but he nodded anyway. Hawley had been an ally at times. Some of it was the job. Anthony understood that. Hawley was paid to hang out with the kids, to praise them and scold them like he was their parent. But Anthony also liked to believe that Mr. Hawley's interest in him was more genuine.

"Not out here," Anthony said as a couple of boys passed between them. He followed Hawley into his apartment, took a seat at the kitchen table, and tried to gather his thoughts. So many things seemed to be turning sour that he wasn't sure where to start.

Mr. Hawley sat down across from him and nodded. "It's okay," he said. "Take your time."

Anthony felt the familiar itch in his eyes but wouldn't let any tears fall. Then he swallowed and told his dorm parent what had just happened upstairs. "On top of that, this man in town shouted the N-word last week," he continued. "Right in front of me and a whole bunch of other people, and nobody said a thing . . . I don't know, Mr. Hawley. I might need to get out of here before I go off on somebody."

Hawley nodded. "This might be Maine, Tony, but sometimes it can feel like the Deep South. Wish I could tell you something different, but I'd be lying to you." He paused. "Why do you even care about some stranger's opinion, anyway? A guy like that lives in a trailer park and marries his kid sisters; he doesn't have any kind of power over you or your life."

"Then what about Mr. Voght?" Anthony said. "Should I care about him?"

Hawley fidgeted. "That's a tough question," he said, looking down. "Want some coffee? I just made it, less than an hour ago."

"Sure." Anthony nodded and checked himself in the microwave. He was wearing a bowling shirt with the name David stitched above the breast pocket. Reflected, it said ᗡIVAᗡ, but it still kind of made sense. Almost everything else in Anthony's life was backward, too.

"Are you excited about vacation?" Hawley asked, bringing over the two steaming cups. "Only about three weeks away."

Anthony solemnly spooned his sugar. "I know. Three weeks." His mother had called a few nights before, crying that she was too broke to buy a plane ticket. She had wanted him to ask if he could stay at his roommate's house again, but so far Anthony had avoided asking Brody. "I might go somewhere different," he said. "Other than home."

Hawley blew on his cup and took a sip. "Someplace warm, I hope."

"Yeah," Anthony said. "Maybe." He stirred his coffee and thought about spending spring break in Lewiston, watching out for Brody's fanatical father and his Somali shack.

"Why did so many people from Africa move up here?" Anthony asked. "I mean, is there something special about this part of Maine that's better than everywhere else in the country?"

"I don't know," Hawley said. "But they're here, and the town is starting to show its true colors because of it."

They sipped their coffee, and Anthony thought about the supermarket cashier; the men sitting in the convenience store; even Brody's father. Their hatred seemed to be more focused on culture than skin color. For a brief second, Anthony felt a twisted hope. "So it's just a Somali thing?"

Mr. Hawley nodded. "Yeah, and a black thing, a Muslim thing, an immigrant thing; they have a thing against anyone who isn't white American."

"Why do so many white people hate us so much, when we haven't done a damn thing to them?" Anthony waited for Mr. Hawley to answer, but he kept on drinking his coffee. Either he didn't know the answer or didn't want to share it.

"I think I know why," Anthony continued. "I think some of them believe that they're supposed to be superior. They think they're supposed to be smarter and richer, live in better houses and everything. When they fall short of all that, they try to blame it on black people so they don't feel so bad about themselves. . . .

It's sad, when you really think about it. Expecting to go out and be the king of the world, but ending up stuck in East Armpit, Maine."

Mr. Hawley smiled across the table at him and shook his head. "Why can't you put that kind of thought in your writing, Tony?"

Smiling back, Anthony said, "Because you don't ever ask the right kinds of questions."

Hawley laughed and went to fill his cup again. But when he sat back down, his face was sober. "Does the name Matt Hale mean anything to you?"

Anthony thought for a second and then shook his head. "Is he a senior?"

"He's an asshole," Hawley said. "And no, he never went to Belton."

He said Hale was a white supremacist who had come to Lewiston a few years back, to try and lead a protest against the Somalis. There'd been a small march, and someone threw a pig's head into a mosque, but most of the Lewiston residents had ignored him. "He's in jail now," Hawley continued. "Somewhere out west, I think. But the point is that some of those marchers still live around here. And with the job situation the way that it is, and with more and more Somalis moving into Hoover . . . I don't know, some people are getting fed up."

"But I'm not from Somalia," Anthony said. "I'm American, just like Brody."

Hawley sipped and smiled sarcastically. "You really think that matters?"

It didn't, and Anthony knew it. African American or African in America, it didn't make any difference to some. He caught his reflection in the microwave again. How many used bowling shirts had Brody handed down to him? It didn't matter if he let people call him Tony, Ant, or Anthony; it didn't matter if his shirts introduced him as David, Chuck, or Steve. Anthony knew that when he turned away, some people would still call him "nigger."

ELEVEN

FOR SPRING BREAK, BRODY'S GRANDPARENTS surprised their family with a trip to Florida, leaving Anthony with no place to go and a hysterical mom. But Mr. Hawley came to the rescue with Greyhound tickets to Cleveland, insisting that Anthony go home and try to forget about the last couple of weeks.

The trek took twenty hours, but Anthony never lost his excitement. He would spend time with his family and hang out with Floyd and Reggie, maybe go the rec center during open gym and show off his new skills in basketball. It would be different than Christmas, when the gap between his two worlds had caught Anthony off guard. This time, he would settle back in seamlessly because now he knew exactly what to expect.

But when his mother picked him up at the bus station and drove home through their dying city, Anthony locked his door and counted the days until he would go back to Maine.

That week, he stayed inside the house, avoiding his friends and wondering why. It wasn't like he didn't miss them. At night up in Maine, especially lately, they were constantly in his thoughts. But on his second day home, Anthony had seen Curtis at the supermarket and ducked down an aisle to avoid him. At the time, he had tried to tell himself that it was no big deal. Curtis wasn't his real friend, anyway. Anthony just hung out with him sometimes because he was Reggie's brother. Deep inside, though, he knew that there was more to it than that. If it had been Reggie standing there instead of Curtis, Anthony probably still would have done the same thing.

One night Anthony was at the table and going over ideas for his speech when he answered the ringing phone and heard Floyd's voice. They hadn't talked since his first day of spring break, and the guilt hit Anthony like a truck.

"W'sup, playa?" Floyd asked, laughing. "I was start-ing to think you jetted to Maine already."

"Naw, man. I'm still here. What's the word?"

"Same old same old, nigga," Floyd answered. "You know what's up. We over here at Reggie's house right now, getting chewed. You should come on over and crack a brew with niggas."

"I don't know," Anthony said, looking at his scribbled notes. "I'm working on something for school."

"School?" Floyd repeated. "Come on, dawg. I thought you was on vacation?"

"This is a speech, not homework. I'm trying to get this job for next year. It's pretty important."

Floyd sniffed. "Pretty important, huh? And you don't think this is? You need to stop staying up in the house every day, like you scared or think you better than everybody else. For real, man. I be trying to stick up for you and everything, but to tell the truth, some-times you be making it hard."

"I am scared," Anthony admitted. "Every time I come home, I get more and more shook."

"Scared of what? Nigga, you from here. Ain't nobody gon' mess with you."

Anthony thought about Mookie. "Yeah, people never get shot in their own neighborhood. . . ."

"You know what I mean, dawg," Floyd said. "Don't try and twist shit up."

"Whatever. I'm not just talking about that, anyway. There're things in this world that scare me more than getting murdered."

"Like what? I gotta hear this one."

At first Anthony didn't say another word. He didn't want to come across as soft. But if he didn't answer, Floyd would think he was lying. "I don't know, man," Anthony said. "Scared of losing my boys. Scared that school is gon' change me too much, to the point where you don't wanna hang out with me."

Floyd grunted. "You trippin'. If niggas didn't wanna hang out, we wouldn't be on the phone."

"All right, man. You win." Anthony put down the pen and closed his notebook. "Save me a brew."

He went over and had fun with his friends, sometimes feeling like a stranger but never unwelcome. It was a good night, and Anthony went to bed with a fantastic inner peace. Then, in the morning, his mother called him into her room and pulled his guts out.

"You know you cain't go back to that school next

year, right?" she said. "We cain't afford it no more."

Anthony sat down on the edge of her bed and stared. "What?"

"You heard me," she said, and pressed buttons on the remote. "We broke."

"But I got a full scholarship," he said, standing up. "My work-study should be covering the books, and I gave you money last summer from the barbershop."

She turned the TV off and looked at him. "That little piece of change you gave me wasn't enough to pay no bills. I still owe that school damn near three thousand dollars."

He was stunned and pissed and didn't try to hide it. "Wait a minute. I thought that—"

"Wait a minute?" she said, cutting him off. Then she kicked the pillows away from her and shot up out of bed. "*Wait a minute?* Boy, who you think you talkin' to? I'm your momma. Don't you ever tell me to wait for anything, you hear me?"

"Yes."

"What?"

"I said yes, ma'am . . ."

She glared, and for a second he thought that she might smack him. If she did, he would leave and never come back again. "Look at you!" she said. "You done gone up there with all them white folks and lost your mind. They got extra charges and fees for every little thing that you do. Maybe if you stop buying those silly-ass shirts we would have some more money to work with."

"I got these from my roommate, Ma. For free."

"There you go with that smart mouth again. That's why you need to bring your black ass back home, anyway. Learn some manners." She waited and then Anthony apologized. After that, she rolled her eyes. "If you wanna blame somebody, blame your daddy," she said. "He supposed to be paying your child support, but I ain't seen a damn dime."

Anthony closed his mouth and held it that way, keeping his face blank. It wasn't just his father's fault that they didn't have any money. What about her cigarettes and VSQ? What about her trips to the beauty parlor and all of her fucking scratch tickets?

"Don't look at me like that," she said. "You got a good year from that school. Coming back to Shaw ain't gon' kill you."

"How do you know that?" he snapped. "When was the last time you went up there, 1980? It's not even the same building anymore, Ma. You don't even know what you're talking about."

She said something to him then, but he wasn't listening anymore. The wheels were already spinning in his head. He couldn't go to Shaw. Not now. Not after a year in a prep school, living with people like Brody. He would call Mr. Kraft and ask for more financial aid. He would get a job at one of the shops in Hoover. One way or another, he would come up with the cash to finish what he'd started. He was already too far gone to turn around and come back.

An hour later, Anthony was stomping down the sidewalk, trying to look menacing but secretly afraid. His mother didn't have the money but that didn't mean that he couldn't get it, just as long as he didn't mind breaking the law.

He met Floyd in front of the building and followed him up the narrow staircase to the apartment that he now shared with his cousin. No one else was home at the time, but they kept their voices low. "That's messed up," Floyd said after he heard about the tuition trouble. "Ain't no way they can let you slide for a while?"

Anthony shook his head. "It's time to pay up or pack my shit in a couple of months." He thought about his reason for coming to see Floyd. It still wasn't too late to change his mind, but he couldn't think of an alternative. "So like, if you put me down with your man," Anthony said. "How long would it take for me to make what I need?"

Floyd scowled, but then he chuckled. "You gon' sell dope, Ant?"

"I'm serious."

"Yeah, right. You serious as cancer." He laughed again, and it made Anthony want to run away or take a swing.

"Look," Anthony said. "If you don't wanna help me, I can go holler at Shane myself."

"Shane?" The bigger boy smiled sadly and shook his head. "Shane been in Lakeview damn near four months, nigga. Only way you gon' talk to him is through a Ouija board."

Anthony closed his eyes. When he opened them, nothing had changed. "Shane is dead? How?"

"Two to the dome. No witnesses." Floyd looked Anthony up and down. "Man, what the hell is you wearing?"

Anthony checked his reflection in the mirror and almost dropped. He had rushed over there in a bowling shirt and Birkenstocks.

"No offense, bruh," Floyd continued. "But how you gon' be on these streets, wearing this bullshit?"

His friend was right, and for so many different reasons. Anthony suddenly wanted to peel off his sandals and throw them through the window. Who the hell was Tony Ohio when it came to East Cleveland? Maybe Floyd would lend him different clothes to wear on the walk back home. "Well, I guess it's back to E.C. and Shaw," he said despondently. "You can show me around, right?"

"Don't look at me, nigga. I ain't been inside that school in a *minute*." Floyd laughed, but he didn't sound happy. "Been too busy chasing that paper."

Anthony looked at the street below. It was sunny and warm, but no one was outside. "Yeah? How soon before you can chase it to a different city?"

Floyd grimaced. "Not for a while. My momma still got another two months in jail, and she gon' have to see a parole officer for a while after that. . . ." He sighed. For a second he seemed much older. "I ain't never told nobody this before, man," Floyd said. "But you the only dude I know who done actually been somewhere."

"You cain't really count Maine as somewhere," he said. "The whole state is just one big, boring forest."

"Yeah, but you *seen* all them trees, man. And you seen New York and Boston, too. You done climbed mountains, drove snowmobiles, stayed in rich people's mansions, with waiters and butlers and shit. How many niggas around here can say that? How many niggas around here can even say they *know* somebody like that?" Floyd clapped Anthony on the back. "Don't take this the wrong way, nigga, but you kinda like a hero to me. Straight up."

Anthony fought a strong urge to hug his best friend hard. Floyd may have teased him about Maine over the months, but it was clear that he'd also been listening. "Stop tripping," Anthony said. "I ain't no hero, man. You are. You already got your own apartment and pay your own bills. . . . Shit, I've been up there wasting time while you've already started living."

Floyd waved his hand. "If you wanna call it that. But I'm just grinding the same way my daddy did, the same way a whole buncha other dudes been doing for the longest. I could die tomorrow or live to be a hundred and never be nobody different than who you looking at, right now. I ain't never gon' make a name for myself except for around here, where a nigga with a name don't last long." He pinched Anthony's bowling shirt between his thumb and forefinger, rubbing the polyester like it was expensive silk. "But you done already made something new outta yourself. David."

"Yeah," Anthony said, looking at his sandals. "And every time I come home, it gives y'all something new to crack on me about."

Floyd chuckled. "Come on, dawg. You gotta admit that some of that junk be funny. Like how you be calling pop 'soda' now, and that bullshit about twenny-five-twenny." He laughed again but then straightened his face when he saw that he was laughing alone. "But niggas still got love for you, dawg. Even Reggie. He be the main one bragging 'bout how his boy fi'n to be a big-time writer."

Anthony made a face, but his friend ignored him. "For real, playa," Floyd continued. "We all be talking about you. When you blow up like Tyler Perry or some shit, everybody in E.C. gon' be like, 'We know him!' But we gon' be like, 'Yeah, but that's our *boy*!'"

Anthony smiled, amazed by the picture Floyd had

just painted because it reflected his dreams. "That's what's up," Anthony said, and then panicked a little. He wasn't even the best writer in his English class. "I'm gonna give it a shot, but I don't know if I'm really good enough."

"You good enough," Floyd said. "Ever listen to yourself tell a story, man? Swear to God, it be just like watching a movie."

"Thanks, man. I needed to hear that."

"Then keep listening 'cause I'm telling you what I feel in my bones." He put a hand on Anthony's shoulder and gave it a little squeeze. "Look, I know we don't hardly be hanging out no more. You got your thing up at that school and I got my thing, right here. Both of us done changed a lot, but that don't mean we ain't still boys. I can go five years without even seeing you and still call you my best friend. You know that, right?"

"Yeah," Anthony said. "I know."

"Good. Then that's why you gon' let me help. Come and see me in a few days, and I should have some cash for you."

Anthony shook his head. "Don't do that, man. You don't have to do that."

"I know I don't have to, playa. I want to. Believe me, it

won't be a whole lot, anyway. My cousin's rent is due."

Anthony went home and sat on his porch. Cars rolled by, blasting music. Kids pedaled bikes across lawns and off curbs. Girls walked in groups, trailing perfume behind them; boys walked in packs, spreading fear. He had two more months at Belton, and then it would be over. Two months before he came back to East Cleveland for good.

Floyd came by a few days later with four hundred dollars in a brown paper bag. Anthony thanked him but wouldn't accept it, saying that his mother had hit the lottery. He spent the last night of the long vacation on the couch and mostly alone. On the news, there were more stories about murders and robberies. Some of them had happened in his neighborhood, but Anthony didn't recognize the victims.

Rolling away from the bus terminal, Anthony watched his neglected city scroll by and wished he was in an airplane instead. From the sky, he would only see shrinking rooftops and neat streets. He wouldn't see the rotten yards and liquor billboards; wouldn't be able to tell the difference between the red boys and the blue ones, the white from black or rich from poor. From the clouds, he wouldn't hear the gunshots, shouts, and sirens, and he wouldn't see shrieking mothers fighting through yellow tape. From way up in the sky, everything below was as pretty as a postcard. But from where he sat inside the northbound bus, everything to Anthony looked bleak.

TWELVE

BACK AT BELTON, ANTHONY DID WHAT HE COULD
to fall into a normal groove. He went to all his classes
and hung with his friends, joined the freshman lacrosse
team and became a pretty good defenseman. As the
days grew longer and warmer, kids talked more about
the upcoming summer. Seniors found where they'd
be going to college, underclassmen paired with bud-
dies and picked their rooms for September. Anthony
decided not to tell anyone that he wouldn't be coming
back. He didn't want to have to explain that his family
was broke.

So he chose Brody for his sophomore roommate, in
case he wasn't voted a proctor, and he left the kitchen

dish crew that spring to work for Mr. Kraft in the admissions office. Anthony also wrote a short story for the literary magazine that Mr. Hawley called "raw and inspiring." Mr. Hawley offered to help try and get it published in a book of teen writers. In many ways, it was Anthony's best stretch at Belton. The better it got, though, the more difficult it was going to be for him to say good-bye.

And then one morning, while sitting in one of the bathroom stalls, Anthony relieved himself and read all the new graffiti. In black marker were the words WHY ARE YOU READING THIS WHEN THE JOKE IS IN YOUR HAND? And another one in red warned to PISS IN SPURTS! MAINE CRABS CAN SWIM UPSTREAM! He laughed and flushed, put his hand on top of the swinging door, and was about to push it open when he noticed another slogan, written in pencil, just above the sliding lock.

NIGERS SUCK

Anthony sat back down. Another freshman had written that, knowing that Anthony and Paul would see it. But who was bold and hateful enough to write it? Most of the boys on his floor marched around in Barack Obama T-shirts.

Rage took over, and Anthony kicked the stall open.

Then he kicked the door again and again, until it hung from bent hinges. Curious faces pressed into the bathroom, and Anthony thought about kicking them, too. "Move!" He stormed into the crowd and the boys fell into one another, trying to avoid him. Seconds later, Anthony was knocking on Mr. Hawley's door.

"You need to see this," he said, and brought Mr. Hawley to the bathroom, where the boys were gawking at the ruined door and misspelled slur.

"Well," Mr. Hawley said, inspecting the writing. "Whoever it was, he's not the brightest bulb in the box."

"I want to know who did this," Anthony said. "I'm serious, Mr. Hawley. These people don't know who they're messing with."

Mr. Hawley tried to calm him, but Anthony kicked the door again. "I can't believe this shit!"

Hawley looked at the dented door and then at Anthony. "Are you finished with that?"

"With that," Anthony said. "Let me catch who wrote that bullshit and I'll stomp on him instead."

Hawley crossed his arms and sighed. The disappointment on his face was obvious. "You can't make those kinds of threats around me, Tony, even in a situation like this. People need to know they're safe around you."

"Safe around me?" Anthony kicked the door off the final hinge. "What about me being safe around *them*?" He glared at Mr. Hawley. "Do what you gotta do, man," he said. "But don't expect me to just shrug this shit off."

For the next few days, things were tense among the students. Gloria and a few other black kids filed complaints. Dr. Dirk called a schoolwide diversity assembly and gave a presentation about the dangers of hurtful words. Some of the kids listened attentively, but a lot of them did homework. And others were offended. They didn't understand why they all should be punished because of one person's stupidity. The school administration was only making things worse by forcing them all to address it.

"Typical!" Gloria shouted without raising her hand. Then she stood up, and a lot of the students sighed. "Just stick your heads in the sand," she said. "Act like it never happened."

"We want to," someone yelled, "but you won't let us!" A few kids laughed and some even clapped until Dr. Dirk warned them to quiet down.

"We'll never make any progress on this if we don't behave with civility to one another," the headmaster said. "Let's use this unfortunate incident as a teaching moment and a chance to come closer together."

Anthony went to his room after that, with Brody close on his heels. "I'm sorry, dude," his roommate said, slowly pushing the hair back from his eyes. They were green. It was the first time that Anthony had noticed.

"Sorry for what," Anthony said, thinking about the antagonism at the assembly and how it all had felt directed at him. "You didn't do anything."

"I know, dude, but still . . . I'm just sorry."

Anthony could tell that Brody was mad about the whole scene, too. But his roommate was white, and nigger was a black word. He didn't want or need Brody's empathy. He didn't want his condolences, his pity, or his sympathetic anger. What Anthony needed more than anything in the world at that moment was the company of other black people.

"I'll be back."

He went down to Paul's room and found Khalik already there. Neither one looked surprised when Anthony walked in and closed the door behind him.

"Assembly got you buggin', too?" Khalik asked, leaning back against the desk.

"Yeah," Anthony answered. "Bugging hard." He told them about his brief exchange with Brody, how his roommate's attempt to understand had only pissed him off.

Paul slammed a fist on his desk. "What does big George call them? Twenty-five-fifty or something like that?"

"Twenty-five-twenty," Anthony said, remembering how mad George had been that day in the kitchen, but also how he had mugged for the crowd at the auction. "I wonder what he has to say about all this?"

"He's pissed," Khalik said. "What you think?"

Anthony hesitated but then said it anyway. There was no use in holding his tongue anymore. "I don't know what to think about your boy," he said. "I used to think he was gaming on these white people, but now I'm not so sure."

"What you mean?" Paul asked defensively. Over the course of the basketball season, he and George had grown close.

"I don't know." Anthony looked at the floor to find the words. "He's just real slick. He does all this stuff to kiss up to the white people and tells us that he's doing it to get over on them. The more I think about it, though, the more I think the dude is kissing up to them for real, and he's really running game on us."

"Game on us for what?" Khalik asked. "What we got that he need?"

Anthony thought and stuck out his arm. "We got this. All the white kids in the world can love him to death, but he knows we're the only ones who can judge him. He needs us to stay in his corner so he can keep believing himself."

Khalik grinned and looked at Anthony. "Sort of like how you used to be, huh, Tony Granola? I see you stopped wearing all those crazy clothes since you went home. Somebody must have said something to you, huh?"

"Something like that." Anthony had traded his bowling shirts for Phat Farm and Rocawear, switched one type of uniform for another. But the clothes didn't define who he was on the inside, any more than the color of his skin. "Let me ask you guys a question," Anthony continued, "and really think about it before you answer. If you could be home in Brooklyn right now, hanging out somewhere with all your friends, would you go or stay right here?"

Khalik sniffed. "What kind of stupid-ass question is that?"

"An important one," Anthony snapped. "Here or at home?"

Khalik drew a breath to say something else, but Paul spoke up first. "I know what you're getting at, man. I wonder that same stuff myself, sometimes."

Khalik made a noise and then started laughing, but the other two boys stared him down. "Don't front, son," Paul continued. "I know the truth." Holding an imaginary phone to his ear, he did his best to imitate the heavy boy's high voice. *"Yo, P, let me come and chill at your spot, man. Niggas around my way is on some other shit."* He laughed and the other boys laughed along with him, but it only seemed to make the mood darker.

"I don't know," Anthony said, thinking about his lost friends, his family, and all the red boys hanging on the corners. "Sometimes I don't feel like I belong at home anymore."

The other boys looked down. Khalik cleared his throat but didn't say anything.

"I know," Paul said solemnly. "The whole time I was home, I couldn't wait to get away. Everything was different, even though it was the same." He crumpled a piece of paper and flicked it toward the trash can across the room. He missed badly, but no one made a comment.

"But I don't feel like I belong here, either," Paul continued. "So tell me, where in the hell am I supposed to go?"

The following Saturday, Anthony went into town with Brody and Nate. They ate pizza and talked about the bathroom stall, which was still a big topic at school. "Call me an asshole," Nate continued. "But don't you think they exaggerate, sometimes?"

Anthony knew that by "they," Nate was talking about the other students of color. But he also suspected that his friend wasn't trying to be offensive. "Maybe sometimes," Anthony said. "But that word is pretty straightforward. You can't say that the person didn't know what he was writing."

"Yeah," Nate agreed. "'Niger.' Maybe it was one of those Korean kids and not even a white person. Ever think about that?" Nate glanced at Brody, who wouldn't look back at him. Anthony knew then that the two of them had been talking about it. "And even if it was a white kid," Nate continued, "crap like that assembly last week does more harm than good. I don't even think about skin color until somebody forces me to."

"Maybe that's part of the problem," Anthony shot back. "People like you have that luxury, but I have to think about it all the time."

Nate raised his eyebrows. "What do you mean, people like me? If I said something like that, I'd be a racist." He looked at Brody again, whose cheeks were turning red. Suddenly Anthony wanted to fly across the table at both of them.

They finished their food and left. It was getting dark, and most of the shops were closing. "Let's go," Anthony said. "Something doesn't feel right."

Brody quickened his pace. Nate called them pansies but walked faster than both of them. They rounded the bend and saw the still-distant campus just as a strange sound grew behind them. Anthony thought about Mookie, turned around, and walked backward, watching the curve in the road. "You guys hear that?"

The boys listened and Nate shrugged. "So what? It is a public road, you know?" They walked on and hit the edge of campus and all its twinkling lights. But then a different kind of light from behind them turned the boys around. The yellow glow bounced off the road and trees like the dazzle from an ambulance. Instead of a siren, though, the boys heard footsteps.

"What the hell is that?" Nate stepped back into the road and squinted. The light drew closer and more intense, and then they saw what was coming: ghostly figures, pulling a wagon that carried a burning cross.

At first Anthony thought he was asleep. Everything suddenly had the slow-motion quality of dreams. He moved closer as the parade approached and saw a figure with a can of lighter fluid dancing around and squirting the flaming wood. He saw the blue jeans and work boots underneath their white robes, the homemade hoods with uneven eyeholes. He had to be asleep because this couldn't be the Klan. Not in Maine. Not walking right in front of him.

"What's the matter, monkey boy?" one of them shouted. "Want a banana?" The man grabbed his crotch and hooted. Soon the rest of the marchers fired insults.

"Put that nigger back on the boat!"

"Take your AIDS back to Somalia!"

Brody hollered, "He's from Cleveland, you fucking assholes!"

"Cleveland?" one of them shouted back. "That's even worse!"

Something about the voice broke Anthony's trance. He started after them, but a speeding truck reached the marchers first. They planted the sputtering cross in the side of the road and piled inside the pickup. Then they sped off down the black strip of state highway, hooting as their taillights faded.

Brody yelled and kicked the cross over. More Belton kids and faculty spilled out into the street. Some of them shouted and a few even cried, but most stood in subdued little clusters.

Anthony looked at the road stretching out into darkness, strained his eyes for signs of the pickup. If it came back again, he'd be waiting with rocks.

The truck never returned, though, and the kids went to their dorms. Frustrated, Anthony broke a window along the way. He liked the sound, so he broke another one. Later that night, Mr. Hawley poked his head into the room. Brody was asleep, but

Anthony wasn't. "Hey, you busy?"

"Nope," Anthony said, getting up. "I figured somebody would come here, sooner or later."

They went to Hawley's apartment and took familiar seats. "So how are you?" Hawley asked. "I can't sleep, especially after what happened."

"What did happen?" Anthony asked. "I was right here and I'm not even sure, myself."

Hawley took a deep breath. "There was a meeting the other day up at the town hall," he said. "Some people want to make it illegal for any more Somali families to move here. I know," he said as Anthony made a face. "You would think it is 1968. Anyway, it got ugly when they couldn't get enough support. And I guess some people got the idea to send their own kind of message."

"By coming down here and burning a cross?" Anthony said. "What kind of sense does that make, Mr. Hawley? We don't even have any Somali students."

"I know," he said. "They started on Birch Street and ended right here, the only two places in town where they can find black people. . . . From what I could tell, they weren't really even the Klan, just a bunch of drunk rednecks, being stupid."

"Rednecks being stupid, huh?" Anthony said. "So I guess next you're going to tell me it was wrong for me to get mad?"

"At them, no. But why did you have to go and destroy school property? Belton didn't have anything to do with what happened."

"Maybe not the march," Anthony snapped, "but plenty of other stuff."

"But breaking windows isn't the answer, Tony."

"Well, what is the answer then, Mr. Hawley? Tell me, 'cause I wanna know!" He hadn't meant to shout, but it made Anthony feel better.

Mr. Hawley rubbed his temples and spoke evenly. "I don't have the answer either, but being a proctor next year can help. Sometimes the best way to change something is from the inside out."

Next year. Anthony thought about telling him that he wouldn't be back, that Hawley would have to look for someone else to help him run the freshman floor. But then Anthony thought about the bus tickets and kept his mouth shut. He didn't want Mr. Hawley to try to rescue him again. Besides, he wanted the opportunity to speak his mind in front of everyone, to get some things off his chest in a way that would be memorable. Most of all, though, Anthony wanted to go through the process and be told that he was good enough. It wouldn't exactly be a Belton diploma, but it would have to do.

On Monday there was another healing assembly, and then Anthony met with the disciplinary committee. At first they voted to suspend him for three days, but he couldn't afford to go back home. As a compromise, they grounded him to campus for a week and made him see Dr. Milton, the school counselor.

When they met, the bald doctor shook Anthony's hand and asked him to have a seat. Anthony relaxed a little and complied. Until then, he had thought he would have to lie on a couch. "Good to see you, Tony," the doctor continued. "Glad you could make it."

"Good to be here, Dr. Milton, but I don't go by Tony anymore. Call me Anthony, or Ant for short."

"No more Tony?" Dr. Milton made a face and then shrugged. "Maybe later you can tell me why you made the change." He pulled out two Cokes from a little refrigerator and gave one to Anthony. Then he popped his can open, sipped, and stared.

Anthony opened his soda, too, drank half of it down, and belched. He looked around the office, but there was nothing interesting to see. Soon his eyes found Dr. Milton again, who was staring at him patiently. "So how is this supposed to work?" Anthony asked. "Do you ask questions, or am I supposed to just talk?"

"Whatever feels comfortable to you. . . ." Dr. Milton sipped his cola again and smiled. It made Anthony want to jump up and run.

"They said I had to talk to you because I broke some windows. . . . I don't know. Maybe they think I went too far."

Dr. Milton folded one leg over the other and nodded. "Is that what you think? That you went too far?"

"Yes?"

"You don't sound very sure about it."

"I'm sure," Anthony said. "I realize it now."

Dr. Milton sipped his Coke. "Why now?" he asked. "Is it because you're sitting here with me?"

"It got me in trouble, right?"

Dr. Milton raised an eyebrow. "So you think that this is some kind of punishment?" he asked. "For breaking some windows?"

"It did come from the disciplinary committee."

Dr. Milton laughed, and Anthony heard pity behind it. "You just survived a traumatic experience, Ton—I'm sorry, Anthony. People dressed as the Klan had just marched through campus. You were angry and needed to do something with that anger. Given the situation, I think it was completely understandable. . . . Maybe a little over the top, but understandable nevertheless."

Anthony stared at the man across from him, waiting to hear a catch. When none came, he decided to push it. "So you can tell them that I'm not crazy?"

"You're not crazy. That's my clinical opinion."

"And that's it? I can go now?"

Dr. Milton nodded but looked at him sideways. "You can go, but why are you in such a hurry? We haven't talked about the name change yet."

At first he didn't understand, but then Anthony remembered and laughed. "People called me Ant for almost all of my life," he explained. "Tony was just a temporary nickname that I picked up, up here."

"Temporary?" He raised his eyebrows. "Why? You don't like it?"

Anthony looked at the ceiling and thought. "I used to. But not anymore."

"I see." Dr. Milton made the face again. "Why don't

you like it anymore? Is it related to everything that's just happened?"

Anthony thought awhile longer before saying anything else. He was wary of the way that the doctor was looking at him. "To tell the truth, I never liked it," he said. "People started calling me that from the first minute I got here. It used to drive me crazy. Not crazy crazy," he added quickly. "But you know what I mean." He checked to see if the doctor was following but couldn't tell by his blank expression. "Anyway, I'd introduce myself as Ant or Anthony and they would just call me Tony anyway. Why is that? Why do some people think they know you better than yourself? Why do they want to give you a different name when you've got one already?" He waited, but Dr. Milton didn't say anything. "I guess it's one of those things that comes with privilege," he continued. "In a way, this whole school is just like it. You only let us wear certain clothes and try to make us all think the same way about things. . . ."

"That's interesting," the man said, leaning in. "I'd like to hear more about that. Think the same—as in coming up with the same answers in class, or do you mean it in another way?"

Anthony thought. There were hundreds of examples to choose from, but finally he picked the most recent. "Like these diversity assemblies. It's obvious that a lot of people here don't like it, but we keep on having them anyway. What's the point? The fact is that a lot of people here are racist. They might as well have been marching with those townies. . . . Shoot, for all I know, some of them were."

Dr. Milton frowned. "Is that what you really believe?"

"No. But I could think of a few who would fit right in. . . ."

"Care to share any names?"

Dr. Dirk. Coach Rockwell. Half the student body and probably most of the maintenance crew. "No," Anthony answered. "And you don't really want me to, either. It's all right, though. That's what I'm trying to say. Instead of trying to stuff everybody in the same box, this school should just let people be themselves."

"Interesting." Dr. Milton took another sip from his can and put it back down. "So by your logic, people can write and say what they want. And you shouldn't have become angry over any of it." He made a big show of crossing his legs again. His pleasant smile turned smug.

"Not really," Anthony said. "Maybe I shouldn't have

broken the windows, but I had every right to get mad. If the dudes in the hoods would have stuck around, I could have told them exactly how I felt."

"Break them, instead of the glass?"

Anthony sighed. "I told you I was wrong for doing that, okay? Like I was wrong for fighting McCarthy in the fall. Just because you knock somebody out doesn't mean it's gonna change his mind. But how can I ever have a debate with a person who stays invisible? They should have done it without their hoods on. Now I won't ever know who I'm looking at anymore." He thought about that night again and the familiar voice. Had it been Mark from the supermarket or someone from the pizza place?

Dr. Milton finished his Coke and threw it away. "You do understand what that was really about, right? This is small-town Maine," he said. "They were reacting to a changing demographic." He jumped and seemed to catch himself. "Not to say that their reaction was correct, mind you. Dressing up as the Klan and using hurtful words is wrong and completely unacceptable."

For a couple of seconds Anthony tried to imagine the good doctor under one of those hoods. But all of the men on the march that night had been much taller. "What is it with everybody trying to defend those clowns?" Anthony said. "Mr. Hawley tried to spin it the same way, like they were just a bunch of good ol' boys wearing costumes. I know it's your town and maybe you don't want to believe it really happened. But it did. Just like that word was really in the bathroom; just like the way people acted at the last diversity assembly. Just like a hundred other things that you'll probably try to explain away. Sometimes things aren't that complicated. Sometimes a thing is exactly what it is."

Dr. Milton tapped his chin. He was obviously buying time. But Anthony was tired and had said too much already. Plus the doctor was too smart for his own good. "Let's talk about that," Dr. Milton said finally. "Are you saying that we're all who we are right now? That no one changes?"

"No."

"Then what do you mean?"

"I'm saying that sometimes we don't want to see the ugliness in others because it means seeing what's ugly in ourselves."

"Fascinating. What do you mean?"

"Some other time," Anthony said. "Can I go now?"

Dr. Milton blinked and regained his smile. "Of course. But can we schedule another appointment?"

"Do I have to?"

The doctor shook his head.

"Then no."

THIRTEEN

FOR THE REST OF THAT YEAR, ANTHONY JONES
was a model citizen. He participated in class discussions, did his homework on time, and spoke pleasantly to everyone he encountered. Despite all of that, he remained a pariah. To most everyone at the school, he was that angry black kid again, the one who would rather fight and break things than learn and get along. If it wasn't for Brody and a couple of his dorm mates, he wouldn't have had any white friends at all.

He'd found copies of winning proctor speeches in the library, all of them delivered by popular kids who bled Belton blue and gold. But Anthony wasn't popular, and he wasn't even coming back. What could he say that would win the crowd over and at the same time not be a lie?

He looked down at what he'd started to write and then crumpled up the paper. In the grass next to his spot on the bleachers was a small pile of other failed drafts. A shadow fell across his knees. Gloria was standing there, laughing and shaking her head at the same time. "Somebody looks serious," she said, bending to kiss him. "I tripped on my way up the stairs and you didn't even notice."

"Sorry. Guess I'm in the zone." He covered the blank sheet with his arm but then saw her looking over the railing. "Those are just rough drafts. The real stuff is in my head."

"In your head, huh? More like your ass. If you're going to lie to me, at least try to be more convincing. What's the matter?"

"Everything," he admitted. "Maybe I should just write some typical rah-rah shit and call it a day. I'm sure it would make everybody happy."

"Not everybody," she said, looking at him fiercely. "Forget the rah-rah and bring the raw-raw. These people need to hear the truth."

He tried to give her the pen and notebook, but she

dropped her hands. "If you won't write it down, then tell me," he said. "What's the truth? Because I don't know it."

"Yes, you do. And you can say it better than anybody else. Give it time and you'll find the words. . . ." She crossed her legs and sniffed. "I heard people forget most speeches anyway."

Anthony looked at her. She was wearing the same clothes as the day they'd met, but her eyes were a little darker and her smile not as bright. "So, do you know where you're going next year yet?"

"I don't know," she said. "I looked at this place down in Massachusetts that seemed pretty cool. Still a lot of white people, though."

Anthony laughed. "Why don't you just go on back to Brooklyn and get it over with? You know you and white people won't ever get along."

"I just might," she said, but then her smile faded. Anthony thought he knew what she was thinking. Just like Anthony, Paul, and Khalik, she no longer fit in at home. "Anyway," she continued, "I might give this school a try. It's close to Boston, so at least there'll be some other black people in shouting distance."

"Yeah," Anthony said. "Some brothers." They laughed,

and Anthony felt a brief tug in his chest. He would always wonder how things could have been.

"What about you?" she said. "You still haven't told anybody else? Not even your boy Brody?"

He shook his head. "Not yet. But me and Brody don't hang out that much anymore. I mean, we're still cool, but since all that junk happened, I don't know . . . I guess I kinda closed myself off from him in a way."

Gloria nodded. "I'm sure he understands all that, but you still should tell him about next year. The poor boy still thinks you're gonna be his roommate."

"I know." He tried to think of arguments against it but couldn't come up with any. "Guess I'll go do it right now," he said, gathering his things. "I'm not getting anywhere with this speech, anyway."

He found Brody in the lounge, watching TV with Venus. He gave them the news at the same time, which in a way made things easier. Venus hugged him and promised to stay in touch, but Brody just stared at him.

"When were you gonna tell me?"

"Today," Anthony said. "At this moment. Right now. I would have told you sooner, but I was still holding out hope that my mother could come up with the money."

"What about the school?" he said. "Can't they give you more financial aid?"

Anthony shook his head. "We tried. Believe me."

"This sucks." Brody's eyes were wet and shining, but Anthony pretended not to notice. "Maybe you can come back for junior year? Get a job, save some money. Make it your goal."

"Yeah. Maybe."

"I'm fucking serious," Brody said, and punched him in the arm. "You do it, dude. Or I'm gonna come to East Cleveland looking for you."

"Okay. I will. But you have to make me your roommate. Nobody can leave snot rags on the floor like you."

"Awwww!" Venus put her arms around them. "You guys are sooo cute!"

That night Anthony had the room to himself. Brody had brought Venus home for the weekend to meet his parents. He was almost asleep when he got a phone call from home. It was Reggie, and he didn't sound right.

"Ant? How you doing, man? What's the deal?"

"I'm good," Anthony answered. "What's up with you? I didn't even know you had this number."

"I got it from Floyd," Reggie said. "Off his cell phone. . . ." There was silence, and Anthony was just about to break it when Reggie cleared his throat. "I don't know how to tell you this, but niggas shot Floyd last week. He dead, man. His funeral was yesterday."

In his head, Anthony said a lot of things, asked questions, and demanded answers. But all that drifted out of his mouth was "No."

"It's the truth," Reggie said, sounding annoyed. "We woulda called you before, but didn't nobody have your number except him."

He was stunned, and although they stayed on the phone awhile longer, Anthony didn't say much of anything else. So far the police didn't have any suspects, and they didn't seem to be looking very hard. Reggie and others were asking around, but they weren't having much luck, either. "That's why niggas need you to hurry up and get back," Reggie said. "We need to find out who did it and handle that shit ourself."

Anthony hung up and went back to his room, fought the urge to smash things, wanted to cry but didn't. His best friend was dead, and he had missed the funeral. Floyd was dead and would never come back. The separation that had started almost a year ago was complete and irreversible. Poor Floyd. He had walked the hard road, burned bright on some street corners, and then died on one of them. And now Anthony was expected to hurry back home and help to avenge the killing. But he wouldn't. He couldn't. No matter how much he wanted to, even if he knew the shooter's name and address. He would honor his best friend's wishes and memory, not disgrace them in the way that Reggie wanted.

He went to Brody's desk and threw open the bottom drawer, found the stubby screwdriver and hammer that he kept for hanging pictures, and marched out into the hallway, gripping them like weapons. First he went to the telephone nook and then into the bright bathroom. When he was finished, he let himself cry. After that, he started a brand-new speech.

A week later, he received some good news for a change. Mr. Hawley told him that a teen magazine was publishing one of his stories. But the police in East Cleveland still hadn't found Floyd's murderer, and the two-man cop team in Hoover still hadn't discovered who had planted the cross. Anthony suspected that neither crime would be solved, but for completely different reasons.

★ ★ ★

The time for his speech arrived, and Anthony marched out with the other kids who were running for office. Up for grabs, in addition to vacant proctor positions, were seats on the student council and the academic board. Anthony's mother and Andre were standing in the front row, clapping wildly.

At the podium, Anthony's heart beat hard in his throat. It looked like the whole world was out there, waiting for a speech he hadn't finished until four that morning. One he was sure they wouldn't like.

"Good morning, everyone," he read from one of the note cards. "As you know, I'm only one of a dozen speakers today, so I promise to keep it brief. After all, we know the real big day is tomorrow." Rowdy cheering and applause erupted from the senior section, along with good-natured insults and encouragement. For a second, it was as if the ugly things hadn't happened. He was Tony again, and they were his friends.

"I'm really honored to be here," he continued. "I want to thank you all for showing me the world and for saving my life. That sounds a little dramatic, I know, but that's exactly what Belton did for me. It saved my life. Before I came here last fall, one of my friends was shot in the head. I was there when it happened, and the guy tried to kill me, too. It was then that I decided to come to Belton, away from a violent world that didn't make sense, to a place that seemed a lot like paradise. The other day, I got a phone call from home and found out that my best friend, Floyd, was shot and killed. I missed his funeral because I was here in paradise and they didn't know how to contact me."

His mother gasped, along with most of the audience. He nodded at her, and Andre rubbed her shoulder. "I'd be lying if I told you that Floyd and Mookie were saints," Anthony said. "But they were young and didn't deserve to die like that. . . ."

There were scattered giggles from a few of the students. For some, Mookie's name had muddled the message. Anthony pressed on and ignored them.

". . . Mookie hadn't even started high school yet and Floyd was just fifteen; both of them shot dead because of where they were standing. So yes, when I say that Belton saved my life, I really mean it. You gave me a safe place to study at night, and now I'm ready to take on the rest of the world, armed with everything that you taught me. And you taught me a lot. Like how to find the North Star in the sky, how to build a snow cave and find clean water in the wild. You showed me how bears mark their territory on trees; that moose really are as big as buses, and skunks smell the same everywhere. You gave me good friends like Paul and Khalik. You gave me Gloria and Big George and the other students of color. You gave me Brody and Nate and Alex Sanger, Venus and Alison and so many others. Before Belton, I didn't know a single white person by name. Now I know more white people than I can count."

He paused and looked around at all the faces. Some of them were crying, but most were grinning ear to ear. "I came here hoping to meet Stephen King but got Mr. Hawley instead. He taught me how to write authentic dialogue, and the importance of revision. He taught me how to be a responsible young man who stands up for what he believes in. Before Belton, I used to dream of riding trains to places like Pittsburgh and Cincinnati, but thanks to Mr. Kraft and the financial aid office, I made it all the way here to the top of the map and have friends from all over the world.

"But what people say about free lunches is true. Everything gained has a price. Admissions didn't charge me much cash for my stay, but it still almost cost my identity. I learned early on that there was no room here for me, anyway. Not for Ant Jones from East Cleveland. If I wanted to stay and get along with the people at Belton, then I had to become somebody else. Being black was okay, even cool, but only when it was convenient for others. If I sat with other black kids or wanted to talk about prejudice, then I was the one being racist. So I put on a mask that was so perfectly polished that it only reflected who you all wanted to see. And I wore it around here, night and day, saving my true face for home.

"For a while I thought that the mask made me clever. It gave me the chance to look both ways; it let me be Tony and Ant at the same time. But the thing about wearing that kind of fake face for too long is that some of it sticks and becomes permanent. Especially around the eyes. It changed the way that I look at the world and the way that the world sees me. . . ." He paused and looked out over the crowd. Some of the faces seemed red and disturbed, but at least everyone was listening. There were still a few unread cards in his hands, but he slid them into his pocket.

"I know that this hasn't been a typical proctor speech, but I'm not coming back next year, anyway. My family can't afford it, and neither can I. Sorry if it makes me sound ungrateful, because I really do love this school. Like I said at the very beginning, Belton saved my life. It's just that you can love a place and still want to help to make it better . . . I don't know. A good friend of mine told me that people forget most speeches, so maybe I'm wasting my time. But I hope that the next Ant Jones who comes along gets to keep his name. And I hope that he doesn't have to pay such a steep price for his free education."

Speech done, Anthony stood awkwardly at the podium, said "thank you" too loudly into the microphone, and hurried back to his seat. Someone stood up and started clapping. Others followed until everyone was standing and hooting.

That afternoon, after they cleared out Anthony's room, Maxine forced both of the boys to pee again before they climbed into the rented van. There was a long drive ahead of them, and she only wanted to stop for gas. Mr. Hawley was on hand outside in the parking lot, and surprisingly, so were a few other teachers. "Helluva son you've got there, Mrs. Jones," one of them said, shaking Maxine's hand through the window. "He's going to go far. I can feel it."

"Thank you." She beamed back. "Thank you very much."

Another one stuck his head partway through the window and shouted to Anthony in the back. "Take it easy, kiddo! Can't wait to buy that first book!"

"I'll sign it. See you later."

Ms. Whitlock came over. "I just wanted to meet this spunky young man's mother!" She patted Maxine's shoulder like they had known each other for decades. Although Anthony couldn't see his mother's face, he imagined how it must have looked.

"Thank you," Maxine said, leaning away from the open window. "And who are you?"

"Just Tony's favorite teacher," she said, grinning. "Constance Whitlock. I'm sure he's talked about me?"

"Sure he has . . . nice to meet you! Thank you so much for taking care of my son."

Ms. Whitlock blushed and said that the pleasure was hers. Then she went and stood with a few other teachers, under a tree. "She wasn't my favorite teacher," Anthony whispered. "She was weird."

"Be quiet, boy," his mother hissed. "Here comes another one."

Mr. Hawley came shuffling over to the van. His eyes were red around the edges and his nose was running. "Ms. Jones," he said, pressing her extended hand warmly between both of his. "I can't begin to tell you how much your son has meant to this school, and to me. I'm supposed to be the teacher around here, but I wound up learning a lot from him." He looked back at Anthony, who was trying to act like he hadn't heard anything. "I'm serious," he continued. "Thank you for coming here."

"I'll be back," Anthony said, and forced a laugh. "When I turn twenty-one we can hit a bar and go pick up some women."

"Anthony!"

"I said when I turn twenty-one, Ma. Relax."

Hawley laughed and said he would think about it. Then Andre said something about the long drive ahead, and Mr. Hawley apologized. "Guess you guys should be shoving off," he said. "Make sure to stay in touch." He moved away from the window and joined the others by the tree. Seconds later, Anthony jumped out of the van and gave Mr. Hawley a hug.

"Take care, Mr. Hawley," he said. "Sorry if I offended anybody today, you know, with the speech. I was just trying to speak from the heart."

"Are you kidding me? You don't need to apologize for that. Half the people were crying."

"Yeah, but what about the other half?"

"Relax, Anthony. Everyone was in awe. It took a pretty big pair to say what you said. It was special, and I'm glad I witnessed it." They hugged again, and when they separated, Mr. Hawley's face was wet. "Jesus," he said, wiping his eyes. "You would think I was the one leaving."

"I'm gonna miss you, man," Anthony said. "You helped me grow up."

"You helped me grow up, too," Hawley said. "The whole school. You made a big impression on all of us." He reached out and gave Anthony a playful punch in the shoulder. "Speaking of impressions," Hawley said, "Floyd Mims wouldn't be the same Floyd from today's speech, would he? Because I noticed that somebody practically chiseled 'FLOYD MIMS WAS HERE' into a couple of walls downstairs."

"For real? I don't know about that one, Mr. Hawley, but if a person went through all that trouble, then it must be pretty important, don't you think?"

"I do. Which is why I'm going to make sure that both

of them stay. Even if it means that I have to go over them every year with a screwdriver or something." He winked and Anthony almost cried, but he gave the man one last hug instead.

Minutes later, the van was speeding down the highway, blurring all of the trees.

ACKNOWLEDGMENTS

THIS MIGHT SOUND CORNY, BUT FIRST AND foremost I'd like to thank my mother. She filled our house with books and encouraged me to write stories (I still have the one about the "where-wolf" from the third grade, thanks to you). I want to thank my brothers, Melvin and George, and my sisters, Carla and Karen. Your guidance and support throughout the years has been invaluable. Daddy, you inspire me more than you know. Keep fighting and don't give up. Tap, thanks for everything, man. Over the years, you've taught me a lot. To the rest of my family (too many to name without adding another twenty pages to this book), I love you and thanks for everything.

To the Mims family, the Thompsons, the Jacksons, D. C. Hardy, Phil G., and the rest of E. 133rd St., thanks for being the best friends anyone could ever have. Thanks to East Cleveland for teaching me hard lessons but teaching them well. Thanks to Bob Flanagan, Dick and Debbie Dorhman, Pete and Vicky Rackliffe, Jim and Lucia Owen, Jim Fiske, Clayton Burroughs, and every other teacher who inspired me. To Adam, Craig, Tommy P., Paul, Dino, Dave, and the rest of my friends from Gould Academy, thanks for the memories. And to all of my friends and colleagues at the Cambridge School of Weston, thank you for nineteen wonderful years of support and growth. I can't wait to see what the next nineteen will look like!

To my agent, Jodie Rhodes, thanks for believing in me. To my editor, Phoebe Yeh, thanks for your help and guidance. I can't wait to do this with you again!

Lastly, I want to acknowledge my wife, Ava, for introducing me to a level of love that I didn't know existed. Thank you for keeping me sane, safe, and unbelievably happy. And thanks to our daughter, Olivia, who is the most beautiful baby in the world. I can't wait for her to watch me grow up. . . .